THE DRAGON'S CHANCE

Lochguard Highland Dragons #9

JESSIE DONOVAN

The Dragon's Chance
Copyright © 2021 Laura Hoak-Kagey
Mythical Lake Press, LLC
First Print Edition

Cover Art by Laura Hoak-Kagey of Mythical Lake Design
ISBN: 978-1944776862

Books in this series:

The Dragon's Chance Synopsis

Over the last year, Jake Swift has constantly thought of the one-night stand he had with a beautiful dragon-shifter, one who slipped away silently into the night. Determined to see her once more, he finally manages to arrive in Scotland at Clan Lochguard's gates and asks to see Sylvia. She's as sexy and kind as he remembers, but he soon learns her secret—he's a father, and they have a daughter together.

Sylvia MacAllister has done her best to be a single mother to her surprise daughter. It's not easy, but she's determined to be the best mother possible, especially given how she failed her other children more than a decade ago. When her daughter's father shows up on Lochguard, wanting to be a part of their lives, Sylvia isn't so sure, but she grants him two weeks to see how things go. The trick will be in focusing solely on what's best for her daughter and not getting attached to the handsome human.

Jake tries his best to win Sylvia, despite her doubts. However, between each of their pasts and family drama, a future together seems uncertain. Will Jake be able to convince Sylvia that he wants both her and their daughter? Or will he be relegated to a part-time dad, unable to claim his new family?

The Stonefire and Lochguard series intertwine with one another. (As well as with one Tahoe Dragon Mates book.) Since so many readers ask for the overall reading order, I've included it with this book. (This list is as of September 2021 and you can view the most up-to-date version on my website.)

Sacrificed to the Dragon (Stonefire Dragons #1)
Seducing the Dragon (Stonefire Dragons #2)
Revealing the Dragons (Stonefire Dragons #3)
Healed by the Dragon (Stonefire Dragons #4)
Reawakening the Dragon (Stonefire Dragons #5)
The Dragon's Dilemma (Lochguard Highland Dragons #1)
Loved by the Dragon (Stonefire Dragons #6)
The Dragon Guardian (Lochguard Highland Dragons #2)
Surrendering to the Dragon (Stonefire Dragons #7)
The Dragon's Heart (Lochguard Highland Dragons #3)
Cured by the Dragon (Stonefire Dragons #8)
The Dragon Warrior (Lochguard Highland Dragons #4)
Aiding the Dragon (Stonefire Dragons #9)
Finding the Dragon (Stonefire Dragons #10)
Craved by the Dragon (Stonefire Dragons #11)
The Dragon Family (Lochguard Highland Dragons #5)
Winning Skyhunter (Stonefire Dragons Universe #1)

Short stories that lead up to *Persuading the Dragon* / *Treasured by the Dragon*:

Semi-related dragon stories set in the USA,

beginning sometime around *The Dragon's Discovery / Transforming Snowridge*:

Chapter One

Roughly One Year Ago

Sylvia MacAllister played with the lanyard around her neck and took one last deep breath before entering the large space that would be used for the baking competition. For the next few hours at least, she was determined to be the person she wished to be. Or at least the one she was trying to be for the duration of the restaurant expo in Glasgow.

In other words, she was just a female without her grown children, without the heartbreak of her long-dead mate, without the usual reserve she tended to show around everyone back home.

She was just Sylvia, the female who loved to cook

and run a restaurant. One who was currently surrounded by people who loved to do the same.

However, despite that, the sight of so many people milling about the large room looking for their assigned stations for the competition caused her heart to thunder inside her chest.

Her inner dragon—the second personality inside her head—spoke up. *They don't know who you are. You can be anyone. Enjoy it. Otherwise, what was the point of coming?*

Taking strength from her inner beast, Sylvia murmured, *I'll try.*

After all, she'd only be in Glasgow a few days, so surely she could manage it. Not to mention how not being surrounded by her grown children or her late mate's family made it easier to be all those things she had secretly wished to be—spontaneous, charming, and someone who dared to take risks just because she felt like it.

Nearly almost everyone else in her life, from her children to her friends, were fairly outgoing and charming. Even her mate, before he'd been killed a little over a decade ago, had been able to make anyone laugh or feel special, all without even trying.

It was part of the reason she'd fallen in love with Arthur MacAllister back when she'd been sixteen. That, and he'd made her feel safe and special each and every day.

Arthur. Even after all these years, she still missed him.

Her inner dragon said softly, *He would want you to be happy, to seek out more adventure, even with him gone.*

I know.

Besides, we may not have a lot of time left. We need to enjoy it.

It was true—Sylvia had been diagnosed with a mysterious dragon-shifter illness about a year ago. The doctors were still trying to figure out what was wrong with her, the only clue being her worsening blood test results. But even without those numbers, every day she was more tired, more prone to bouts of depression, and feeling more lost in a storm she couldn't control.

No. She wasn't going to think of that. This weekend was for her and her alone. Aye, she was at the expo because she ran Clan Lochguard's only restaurant, and she liked to see the newest equipment on offer and to find suppliers. However, she was also determined to enjoy herself as much as she could. To try and have a little fun, make her own mischief, and pretend she didn't have five adult children despite the fact she was only forty-three.

She scanned and wandered the giant room filled with hundreds of cooking stations, looking for the table assigned to her, and did her best to calm her thumping heart. As soon as she found her assigned partner for the competition, she'd need to fight against her shyness and be more than quiet Sylvia, the one sitting in a corner more content to watch than talk.

Her inner beast spoke up again. *You have something in common with every single person here. No one would have entered the competition if they didn't like to cook or at least have ties to the restaurant industry.*

Maybe.

The event was open to anyone attending the expo who wasn't a pastry chef or ran a bakery. In other words, it was a lighthearted competition for those who didn't bake professionally.

Her dragon sighed. *Just find our station and focus on our assigned partner for now. Maybe if you talk with him, you'll forget to be nervous. Because if you don't calm down a wee bit, you'll never get to try out this new side of you.*

Sylvia glanced down at her paperwork and read the male's name again—Jake Swift. The only other information on the paper said he was American.

Of course she'd be paired with a foreigner. At least with another British or Irish person, she'd have a lot more in common.

Her beast grunted. *Just stop it. We mated young and never got to travel. I think it's brilliant we have a Yank partner. At least that's something new, and the whole reason you're here is to try something new. Stop making excuses.*

Her beast was right. Standing tall, Sylvia pushed aside both her excuses and her nervousness and walked on, looking for her station.

As she drew nearer the one labeled #88, she noticed a male standing near the counter, with his back turned to her. He had broad shoulders, ginger hair that contrasted with his pale skin, and looked to be a little taller than her.

Then he turned around and she did a double take.

He had a strong jaw, a close-cut beard, and eyes that had crinkle lines at the corners, as if he liked to smile and laugh a lot.

It was only then he looked down at something on Station #88's counter and Sylvia realized that the sexy human standing there was her partner for the event.

That was Jake Swift.

Her dragon hummed. *Good. Charm him and maybe we can have some fun tonight.*

He lifted his gaze and met her eyes. For a second, her heart stopped beating. He had lovely hazel eyes, ones with a tad more brown than green, and they were full of amusement.

It was only then she realized that she'd been standing still with her mouth slightly ajar.

Closing her jaw and taking a deep breath, she forced her legs to work again. It took everything she had to keep her cheeks from heating as she reached the station.

The human male was only about an inch taller than her, and she rather liked they were almost eye level. When he spoke, his deep voice made her stomach flutter. His flat American accent greeted her ears. "Hello. Are you Sylvia MacAllister?"

This was it. Old Sylvia would've mumbled something and stammered a reply. However, she wasn't about to let her momentary gawking earlier ruin her weekend of good fun. She never broke her gaze and kept her voice strong as she answered, "Aye, that's me. Call me Sylvia. Jake, is it?"

He nodded just as her dragon spoke up. *Ask him if he's single.*

Not now, dragon.

She had expected Jake to either be surprised or wary since her pupils flashed to slits whenever her inner dragon spoke and most humans weren't used to it.

However, he merely smiled and asked, "So which dragon clan are you from then? The Scottish one?"

"Aye, Clan Lochguard, which is far up in the Highlands. And since you're not running away in fear, I'm guessing you work with dragons wherever you're from…?"

He smiled easily and Sylvia's stomach did a little flip. "Yeah, I run a series of restaurants in the San Francisco area and sometimes deal with nearby dragon clans. But that's not the sole reason. My cousin works with the American Department of Dragon Affairs and even mated a dragon clan leader herself. I've only met him the once when I had some business in Las Vegas and stopped near Tahoe, but he seems nice enough." He shrugged. "Dragon-shifters are just like humans, for the most part. And to be honest, the flashing eyes is kind of cool, if you ask me." He leaned closer. "Is it rude to ask what your dragon was saying?"

She raised her brows. "If your cousin works with ADDA, I'm sure you know it's rude to ask that."

He raised an eyebrow. "Seeing as you were staring at me and drooling a minute ago, I think it'd make us even."

Her cheeks heated. *Damn.* He'd noticed that.

However, she wasn't about to back down. "I'm sure you're used to people staring at you." Bloody hell, had she really said that? She tamped down her embarrassment, shrugged, and added, "Aye, I stared, but I can promise you I won't jump you and rip off your clothes at any second. There's a competition to win, aye?"

He grinned and lowered his voice. "I think the ripping off clothes sounds like a lot more fun to me."

Was he…flirting with her?

Since Sylvia hadn't done that with anyone but her late mate in more than years, she had no idea.

Her dragon grunted. *Aye, he is. Don't stop now. At this rate, we might get some sex after all.*

An image flashed of Jake over her, pinning her hands above her head with one hand as his other stroked between her thighs, and she did her best to push it away.

Jake's chuckle garnered her attention. "Between the flashing pupils and how red your face is, I think I really, really want to know what your dragon said."

She couldn't help but smile at his teasing tone. "Let's win the competition, and I'll tell you whatever you want about my dragon."

"Anything? Is that a promise?"

She nodded. And as he smiled down at her, playfulness dancing in his eyes, Sylvia's heart beat double-time.

Bloody hell, this human was too handsome for his own good.

For a second, she glanced at his lips. Firm, yet soft and inviting.

What would it be like to kiss him?

Jake put out a hand, as if to shake. "I'll take that deal."

She looked back at his hazel eyes. "You're either quite cocky or really good at baking."

"I can be really determined when I want to be. And I want to know this dragon of yours. After all, it's the more instinctual side of you, right? And that fascinates me."

Oh, dear. Just how much had his cousin shared with this human about dragon-shifters?

Because if they did win and he asked about her beast, she'd feel honor bound to answer him.

Her dragon growled. *Good. Because him naked in bed would most definitely be a mini-adventure.*

She'd never really thought about having sex with another male after her mate had been murdered, not once in the eleven years she'd been a widow.

Until now.

Because something about Jake Swift put her at ease in a way she hadn't felt in a long time.

Placing her hand in his, she nearly sucked in a breath at his warm, firm grip.

He may only be an inch taller, but his hands dwarfed hers.

One of those hands would be more than able to palm her entire breast. And at that thought, her nipples tightened.

Jake squeezed her hand and finally let go. "Then let's make sure everything is here and in working order. Because now I have a reason to win, and pity the fool who stands in my way."

He was just so…confident. Not in an arrogant way, but in the self-assured way of a male who'd worked hard and seen success.

Having more than one restaurant in a place like San Francisco definitely signaled success.

And if she were honest with herself, she rather liked how he was determined to win simply so he could get to know her better.

So Sylvia helped get everything set up. And once the competition started, she and Jake worked together seamlessly, barking orders when needed at each other, almost as if they'd done this a million times before.

Hours later, Jake tugged Sylvia into his hotel room and she squeaked. As soon as he shut the door, he pressed her up against it and said, "Tell me something else your dragon said."

Sylvia's cheeks were on fire, but she didn't care. She waited for her dragon and her inner beast said, *I want to kiss him, shred his clothes, and toss him back on the bed.*

It was the most direct statement by far, bolder than the little flirtations her beast had tossed about. But Sylvia repeated it to Jake, and heat flared in his eyes. "I like that idea." He leaned closer, his breath dancing against her lips. He murmured, "I want to kiss you, Sylvia. Tell me I can."

With his hard, warm body surrounding hers, her nipples throbbed at the same time wetness rushed between her thighs. She itched to pull him close, dig in her nails, and have her way with him. "As long as you know the risk."

He brushed hair off her cheek before kissing her jaw. After worrying her earlobe with his teeth— which made her lean even more against the door behind her—he said, "You told me you had a true mate before, right? It's highly unlikely to happen again."

Aye, a dragon finding two true mates in their lifetime didn't happen often. But it wasn't impossible.

Still, her beast didn't think he was one.

And she rather hoped he wasn't.

Not that she didn't like Jake or want to get to know him better, but he had a life back in America. One that he wouldn't want to give up.

A night of fun, however, would be quite another thing.

And given his hard cock pressed against her lower belly, he wanted that as much as she did. "Unlikely, aye."

Threading his fingers into her hair, he moved even closer. "Good enough for me."

He crushed his lips against hers. No need to claim him for a mate-claim frenzy spread through her body, so she moaned and opened her mouth.

Jake slid his tongue inside, stroking, licking, teasing until she battled with him. As they both tried to dominate the other, Jake lifted her up against him, and she wrapped her legs around his waist.

As he pressed her harder against his cock and front, her nipples crushed against his firm chest. She groaned and took the kiss even deeper, needing to taste him, and drown herself in this male's heat.

The next thing she knew, he laid her on the bed. As he tugged off his clothes, she did the same.

Then he kissed her again, pulled her to the edge of the bed so that her legs dangled off the side, and tweaked one of her nipples with his fingers.

He rubbed his cock back and forth against her clit, and Sylvia dug her nails into his back, hissing at the friction.

If he kept it up, she'd come within seconds.

However, he stood up and looked down at her, stroking his cock with his hand as his burning gaze traveled down her body.

At the approval in his eyes, she grew even wetter.

He ran a finger down her belly, over her hips, and to her inner thigh. As he lazily traced shapes there, she widened her legs, needing more than a teasing touch.

"Jake," she murmured.

He met her gaze and slowly kneeled until his shoulders were between her thighs.

As his warm hands rubbed the inside of her legs, he spread them wider. "I want to eat this sweet pussy, Sylvia. Tell me I can."

His dirty words made her skin even hotter.

Suddenly, all she could think about was his tongue fucking her, teasing her, making her come.

He murmured, "I know enough about dragons that I don't have to worry about diseases." He stroked her once, making her gasp at the slightly rough pad of his finger. "Let me taste you, devour you, make you lose your fucking mind."

If her skin grew any hotter, she'd burst into flames.

And thankfully whatever illness she had only affected dragon-shifters, so she had no reason to deny him.

Not trusting her voice, she nodded.

His hands inched closer to her cunt, but didn't touch. "Say it, love. That way I know you want it."

"Aye, I want it."

Never breaking eye contact, he lowered his head until his tongue licked her slit, and she arched at the warm, wet feeling.

Not that she had many more thoughts as he teased her pussy, her lips, and circled but never quite touched her clit. It both frustrated and aroused her, the way he took his time and kept her on the edge.

Then he lightly flicked his tongue against her clit, and she moaned.

But instead of continuing, he entered a finger into her pussy, slowly thrusting, and she instinctively moved her hips to fuck his finger.

"My sweet Sylvia. That's it. Take what you want, love."

He added another finger, and the fullness made her want more, so she moved faster, trying to get him deeper.

She was lost, chasing her own pleasure. When Jake suckled her clit as he lightly flicked it with his tongue, pleasure exploded. She screamed as her pussy milked his fingers, the slight fullness making the orgasm that much sweeter.

The whole time he continued to stroke her lightly on her clit, her lips, and his light touches kept her dangling in bliss, hovering between pleasure and pain.

Eventually he stopped teasing her, removed his fingers, and she relaxed against the bed. Jake stood, lightly rubbed his lips, and then leaned down to kiss her.

At the faint taste of herself in his mouth, heat fired again in her lower belly.

She wanted much more than his tongue between her thighs.

Jake pulled away and smiled. "Well, I'm guessing we're not true mates then?"

"No," she managed, trying to make her brain work.

Damn the man for turning her brain to mush.

And he'd only used his tongue and fingers.

He reached down into the drawer next to the bed, took out a condom packet, and went to work putting it on. As he did so, something at the back of her mind—from when she'd been a teenager in sex ed class—niggled about human condoms and dragon-shifters, but she couldn't remember why that was important.

Then Jake scooted her back on the bed before

laying between her thighs, and she forgot about everything but the male pressed against her.

She brushed hair off his forehead, and he said, "I have three more, my dragon lady. So let's see if we can use all of them."

He kissed her as he positioned his cock at her entrance. As he entered, she groaned. She may have had five children, but she hadn't had sex in over a decade.

And damn, Jake was big.

He finally planted himself to the hilt but held still, and Sylvia grew impatient for him to move.

Her inner beast spoke up. *Tell him to hurry. Or he might get to meet me and I'll ride him. Hard.*

She dug her nails in his arse and said, "Just a warning—if you take too long, my dragon might take control and claim you herself."

A mingle of heat and anticipation flashed in his eyes. "Promise?"

Her beast hummed. *Aye, I like him. He'll do.*

Not wanting her dragon to think this was more than one night of fun, she pulled Jake's lips down to hers and kissed him.

He rocked his hips, slowly at first, but soon he was thrusting hard, each movement reaching even deeper inside her.

She continued stroking his tongue with her own, digging her nails into his back, and moving her hips to meet each of his thrusts.

Even though she'd just had an orgasm, another was building.

Jake broke the kiss and laid his cheek against hers. "Fuck, Sylvia. You're taking me so deep, clenching me so tight. You're perfect."

She knew it was the lust haze talking, but she didn't care.

His words made her feel beautiful and desired. Something she hadn't felt in a long, long while.

Not wanting to dwell on fanciful thoughts, she squeezed her inner muscles, and Jake groaned. He rewarded her by moving a hand between them and rubbing her clit.

His touch was electric, bringing her even closer until she cried out. Jake claimed her mouth again, swallowing her screams as he stilled and found his own release.

He finally broke the kiss and stared into her eyes, both of them breathing heavily, and she saw tenderness in his expression.

Not wanting to read into that, she smiled. "How long before we can work through the rest of your condoms?"

He grinned, the dimple on one side of his cheek making her insides wobbly. "With you? Not long." He kissed her roughly a beat before pulling back and saying, "I hope your dragon comes out to play soon."

Her inner beast—still dazed slightly from the

orgasm—said, *As soon as he's hard, I'll ride him. That's a promise.*

Sylvia giggled. Jake raised his brows and she repeated her dragon's words.

He took her chin between his fingers, kissing one side of her mouth, then the other, before saying, "Give me a couple minutes to rouse the little soldier and then I'm all yours."

"Little?"

A smug smile came across his face. "And that is exactly how to help me get hard again."

He kissed her and then pulled out. "Stay right there."

Jake dashed into the bathroom and shut the door.

Sylvia smiled and stretched her arms above her head.

Aye, she'd found her adventure at last. And even though it had to end before morning, she wouldn't think about that. Tonight was about fun and pleasure with one of the sexiest males she'd ever seen.

And that was all it could be. Not only because the doctors didn't think she had more than a year or two left to live because of the dragon-only disease—they were positive it wasn't something humans could catch since it seemed to thrive on dragon-shifter hormones —but Jake had a life back home in America.

No, the night would be for fun and only fun, with plenty of pleasure thrown in.

And by the time Jake came back into the room,

she forgot about everything else but the moment. Her dragon took control of her mind and rode him until he squirmed. After two more times—with Sylvia back in control—Jake fell asleep, and she slipped out of bed, gathered up the things in her room, and rushed back to Lochguard in the Scottish Highlands.

Chapter Two

Present Day

J ake Swift pulled his rental car up to the large, metal gates of Clan Lochguard and hoped he hadn't made a huge mistake coming here unannounced.

It had been about a year since he and Sylvia had shared that night together in Glasgow. The one he hadn't been able to stop thinking about.

And not just because of the sex—which had been fucking fantastic—but also because of the teasing during the baking competition all the way through to him holding her once they were exhausted, him falling asleep with the dragonwoman in his arms.

It may have only been one damned day, but he'd never felt so at ease around a woman before.

And yet she'd left before he'd woken up. There'd been no note, nothing.

He'd looked for her the other two days of the expo, but she hadn't been anywhere.

And just as he'd thought about driving up to Lochguard, he'd gotten the call about a kitchen fire at one of his restaurants.

So he'd hightailed it back to San Francisco and dealt with the emergency. He'd thought about flying back to Scotland after that, but then his older sister had received word that her son had been killed during an attack in Afghanistan.

Months had passed as he helped his family through the tragedy, being the shoulder his sister needed to lean on since she'd lost her husband a few years ago, until it'd been about a year since that night. He'd attended the yearly expo again, hoping to see her, but Sylvia hadn't been anywhere.

Maybe some would think him foolish, or desperate, or some other negative description to chase a woman who had left in the middle of the night.

However, Jake liked answers and knowing things for certain. He wasn't a man who liked what-ifs distracting him.

So he'd taken a gamble and driven up to the Highlands of Scotland.

Where he now sat in front of the huge metal gates, emblazoned with the clan's name in twisted metal, wondering if Sylvia would want to see him.

He was a fairly confident guy, but she'd slipped away while he'd been asleep for a reason.

However, his gut didn't think it was because she was married, or anything like that. But there had been sadness and shadows in Sylvia's eyes at times, when she thought he hadn't been looking.

He wished he knew why. Maybe that was the reason she'd fled.

Again, stupid fucking what-ifs.

He'd change that today if it killed him. Even if she turned him away, he'd take it. Not without a little talking first, to find out the reason, but at least he'd know the truth and be able to figure out what came next.

The speaker next to the car came to life, garnering his attention as a Scottish male voice asked, "Who're you?"

"My name's Jake Swift. I'm here to see Sylvia MacAllister."

A brief silence, and then the voice asked, "Is she expecting you?"

He wondered about the three-second pause but pushed it aside. "No. But I do have permission to be here, though. I can show you my paperwork if you let me inside."

His cousin Ashley had pulled some strings for

this visit. Even now, her voice rang inside his head: *"Are you sure about this, Jake? I'm more than willing to pull in a favor for my dearest cousin, but she might not want to see you."*

He'd told her he needed to at least try to talk with Sylvia. And bless his cousin, she'd dropped her questioning and had coordinated what she could, telling him to call her anytime if he needed help with either the UK Department of Dragon Affairs or for any kind of information about dragon-shifters in general.

Of course, if the damn Scottish dragons didn't let him inside, it would all be for naught.

The voice finally ordered, "Drive straight until the first building, turn into the car park on the left, and wait for someone to collect you."

The gate swung inward, and Jake's heart thumped as he followed the directions and parked the car.

As he waited, he resisted running a hand through his hair. Jake wasn't usually nervous about anything, and yet all his fantasies and what-if musings would be decided soon.

He only hoped he'd made the right choice. His gut was great at making business decisions, but not so much with women.

He was forty-three and had never been married. Hell, after his one failed engagement in his early twenties, he'd never again *wanted* to be married, preferring to throw everything he had into his restaurants.

Even so, Sylvia had been so much more than any of the women he'd dated in the past. One day with her had been more life-changing than most of his time with his ex-fiancée.

Let's hope you're not being a fucking idiot and merely thinking with your dick, Jake.

He'd had plenty of time to replay sex with Sylvia. And yes, the orgasms had easily been the best of his life.

But teasing her had been just as fun, as had them barking orders at each other as they'd made their three-tier cake. Not to mention he'd enjoyed playing with her dragon half as well.

Maybe he'd read into everything wrong, but regardless of what happened, he'd made the right choice in coming here. It was better to know for certain than to wonder about what could've happened forever.

A pair of people came out of the building in front of his car—a dragonman and woman, judging by their tattoos. The woman had wild, curly hair and an older baby propped on her hip. The man had brown hair and wore a serious expression. The dragonman motioned for Jake to come out of the car.

Grabbing his paperwork, he did and stood in front of them.

The dragonwoman murmured, "Aye, I thought it had to be him. Seeing him, there's no doubt."

Jake frowned. "Excuse me?"

The dragonman gave the woman a meaningful glance and then focused his intense gaze back on Jake. "I'm Grant, and this is Faye. We're in charge of security here. Now, follow us and we'll talk inside."

The baby—wearing a little sailor dress and cardigan—reached out a hand toward him and Jake smiled. "Hello, little one. Who're you?"

Grant grunted, but the woman spoke before he could. "This is our daughter, Isla. Say hi to the human, Isla."

She waved and the baby mimicked her.

Even though his nieces and nephew were all grown now, he remembered what they'd been like at the same age. He waved back. "Hi, Isla. I'm Jake. Nice to meet you."

Faye whispered, "He sounds funny because he's American. But we won't hold it against him."

Jake snorted, but the dragonman spoke up before he could reply. "Come on."

He waited for Faye to go first, and then Jake followed her, with the intense dragonman coming up behind him.

They passed a few people as they went into the main entrance and down the hall. Everyone stared at him with strange looks, which he didn't understand.

From the small research packet Ashley had given

him, he knew there were other humans living on Lochguard. So he wasn't exactly an anomaly.

Faye opened a door and walked into the room. Jake followed. Inside was a table surrounded by some chairs, as well as a long mirror along one wall. He suspected it was some sort of observation one.

Grant motioned for him to sit. Once they all did, Jake pushed his paperwork toward them. "You can see I'm allowed to visit, if that's your concern. All I want to do is talk with Sylvia MacAllister."

As Grant scanned the documents, Faye asked, "Why?"

He was honest but gave the bare minimum. "We met at the restaurant expo last year and hit it off. She left before I could get her information, and I didn't see her there this year. So I thought to come up here and say hello."

Grant gave Jake back his papers. "Aye, you have the credentials. However, I'll be leaving it to Sylvia as to whether she wants to see you or not." He stood. "Wait here."

Since Jake wasn't entirely sure if Sylvia would want to see her one-night stand again, he hadn't expected anything less.

Grant looked at Faye and raised his brows, but she shook her head. "I'm going to stay here."

"Faye…"

"Give me some credit, Grant. I just want to chat with him."

The pair had some sort of wordless conversation until Grant sighed. "Fine. I'll be back shortly with an answer, and I'll have some tea sent in."

"With lots of biscuits, too," Faye added.

With a nod, Grant left Jake alone with Faye and her daughter.

As she absently bounced her daughter in her lap, Faye said, "So how about you tell me about you and your family?"

And so he answered a series of strange questions as he waited.

SYLVIA FINISHED CHANGING her three-month-old daughter, Sophie's, nappy and hoisted her up against her shoulder. "There, now, you're all clean, lassie. Maybe you'll take a nap for your dear mummy, aye?"

Sophie squirmed a little and drooled on Sylvia's shoulder.

As she lightly patted her daughter's back and swayed gently, she mentally crossed her fingers her bairn would sleep. The last few nights had been a constant battle, with Sophie crying more often than not and Sylvia barely keeping her eyes open.

Her inner dragon spoke. *The doctor said she's fine. She's just a restless one.*

Aye, and more stubborn than any of my other children, which is saying something.

Her dragon paused and then added, *It could be because of her father. Of course we don't know since you haven't bothered to look for him.*

She resisted sighing. *We've been over this, dragon. I don't know where to find him. And the expo organizers said they wouldn't pass a message to another attendee for us, either. Besides, Sophie needs all our attention, aye? She's what matters.*

Sylvia loved all six of her children, but Sophie was her second chance in more ways than one.

Not only had her pregnancy somehow helped cure her illness—Dr. Layla McFarland thought it might have something to do with Sophie's human half since tests revealed human hormones improved results—but Sylvia had struggled to take care of her other five children when her mate had been murdered. Her eldest daughter, Cat, had stepped in to help with the family until Sylvia had been able to drag herself out of her deep depression.

This time around, she was going to devote everything to her daughter. She'd be the mum she always should've been.

Her beast said gently, *You did the best you could. Losing Arthur devastated us both.*

It did, but it still doesn't excuse my actions. Wee Jamie had only been ten at the time.

Jamie was her youngest son. *He's twenty-two now and turned out fine.*

Sophie squirmed and started crying again.

Ignoring her dragon, she sat down and tried feeding her daughter.

When that didn't work, she tried rocking her and singing her favorite lullaby.

And yet Sophie still cried.

"What's wrong, Sophie Rose? Your mum could use a wee clue."

Sylvia debated asking one of her grown children to help for a short while. Maybe then she could take some paracetamol for her pounding headache and try eating something quickly to give her more strength.

However, someone knocked on the front door before she could make a decision.

Doing her best to soothe her daughter—who continued to cry—she opened the front door to find Grant McFarland—one of Lochguard's head Protectors—standing there. "Grant? Why're you here? Is something wrong?"

Sophie wailed louder, and it took everything Sylvia had to not cry herself out of frustration.

She was frazzled and most definitely not fit for company, but she tried to smile at Grant.

Grant put out his arms. "Let me take the wee lass."

Under normal circumstances, she'd ask if he was sure. But between her lack of sleep, her pounding headache, and frayed nerves, she easily surrendered her daughter.

Grant took Sophie and murmured as he tickled her cheek. Miraculously, Sophie stopped crying.

Trying not to feel like a failure, she took a deep breath and asked, "What's going on, Grant?"

He met her gaze and said, "Jake Swift is here on Lochguard, asking for you."

She stopped breathing a second. "What?"

"He's waiting in the Protector building, asking for you. But I said it was up to you whether you'd see him or not." Grant looked pointedly at Sophie and back to Sylvia. "He's the father, aye?"

She saw no point in lying to Grant and nodded.

He continued, "The decision is yours, Sylvia. Tell me what you want and I'll make it happen."

Memories of Jake's smiling face, his ginger hair, his hands wandering over her body all crashed over her.

Part of her screamed to go see him straight away. And yet the other part said no, she needed to protect Sophie. He'd come intending to find only Sylvia, not a daughter he didn't know existed.

Although not telling him seemed wrong. Regardless of what Jake decided, Sophie would stay on Lochguard. She was half-dragon-shifter, and since the gene to shift into a dragon was always dominant, it meant she had to live with a dragon clan.

Sophie was also young enough that she'd never need to know if her father rejected her.

Although Sylvia would know, which was nearly as

bad. Just the thought of having to explain the truth to her daughter when she was older and asked about her dad made her stomach churn.

Even though Sylvia planned to let her daughter constantly know how much she loved her, it may not be enough in the end.

As the room started to spin, she leaned against the doorframe. The lack of sleep and food—when had she last eaten?—was starting to affect her.

Somehow she tamed the dizziness and blurted, "I'll see him."

Grant nodded and held out Sophie. Sylvia reached out to take her, but another wave of dizziness came over her, and she crashed to the floor as the world went black.

Chapter Three

J ake didn't know how long he sat with Faye answering her questions before Grant returned. But instead of Sylvia following Grant into the room, a twenty-something dragonman with dark hair and blue eyes walked in. Something about him seemed familiar, although Jake couldn't place it.

Grant motioned toward the dragonman. "This is Connor MacAllister, Sylvia's son."

He blinked. Her…son?

Well, it wasn't exactly like they'd talked in depth about their lives. But she must've been super young when she'd had this Connor, who looked to be in his twenties.

Connor crossed his arms over his chest and said, "Aye, I'm her son. And whilst my mum said she wants to see you, there's been a hiccup. It was a four-to-one decision amongst my siblings—I was the one who voted against letting you see her—but if you want the chance to visit with my mum, come with me."

He blurted, "Sylvia has five children?"

"Aye, there are five older ones. Want to run now?" Connor asked with raised brows.

Jake wondered about the "five older ones" part of his statement.

But right then and there, none of that mattered. Even if learning about all of Sylvia's children was a shock, it didn't change him wanting to talk with her. He'd been dreaming of seeing her for over a fucking year. He wasn't going to run at the first new bit of information.

Jake stood. "Of course not. Although I hope I can talk to her alone."

Connor's pupils flashed to slits and back to round. "We'll see about that."

Faye stood up and sighed. "You can stop with the macho act, Connor. Just let the poor human see Sylvia. She doesn't need babysitters."

Connor grunted. "I'm the oldest male of the household, and it's my job to protect my mum."

Faye rolled her eyes. "Since when?"

Jake merely cleared his throat, and both sets of eyes turned to him. "Maybe Grant can take me to see Sylvia?"

Connor turned toward the door. "No, you're with me. Now, come on."

He followed the dragonman out of the building and down a gravel path. Jake was nearly as tall as Connor, so it wasn't too hard to keep up. Although, given how dragon-shifters were pretty damn fast, the guy was probably slowing his steps to keep Jake from running.

He took the time to study Connor. The young man was nearly half Jake's age, which brought him back to wondering just how young Sylvia had been when she'd had kids.

Then other questions started flying through his head. Was she married? Seeing someone else? Had the night in Glasgow meant the same to her as it did to him? Had his gut been wrong about her?

Stop it. He'd find answers to all those questions soon enough.

As they passed more stone cottages and other dragon-shifters—an older woman stopped in her tracks and openly stared at him before murmuring something to the older man next to her—he got the feeling there was something going on that they weren't telling him.

He was attractive enough, sure. But he wasn't a movie star lookalike or anyone famous. There was no reason for people to notice him.

Another older dragonwoman walked up to him and blurted, "Are you finally here to see Sophie?"

Jake frowned. "Who's Sophie?"

Connor growled. "Shut it, Meg, and move along."

"Well I never, Connor MacAllister. I'm going to tell your granddad about this."

"Go ahead. Now excuse us. We have something to do."

At the furious look on Connor's face, a prickling of unease crept up his spine. Had Sylvia even been her real name, or was it just an alias? "Who is this Sophie person?"

"That's not for me to say."

Jake's temper didn't flare often, but it was starting to heat up. Obviously they all were keeping a secret from him.

And yet, he did his best to take deep breaths and calm himself. Exploding wouldn't help anything right now.

By the time Connor waved ahead of them and said, "There's my mum's house," Jake was almost rational again.

They were about three feet from the door when it opened, revealing another dark-haired, blue-eyed dragonman who looked too much like Connor to be a coincidence.

He must be another son.

The dragonman at the door said, "At least you brought him here in one piece. I was worried you might need to prove how big your dick is by slicing off a few limbs."

Connor growled, "Don't push me, Ian. He's in one piece for Mum's sake."

Ian looked at Jake and raised his brows. "Well, I see now why everyone's been sending me text messages. It's obvious."

Jake clenched his teeth a second and somehow made his voice even when he asked, "What's obvious?"

A familiar female voice drifted from somewhere inside the house—Sylvia's. "Can you two be nice for a change and just show him inside, aye?"

Ian stepped aside. "I have no problem with the human. It's only Connor who's acting like an arsehole."

Not wanting to get in between the brothers, Jake walked past Ian and down the hallway the man had gestured toward. He soon came to a doorway and looked inside.

Sylvia sat on a sofa, a blanket settled across her lap and a mug in her hands. She had the same blue eyes and dark hair he remembered, although she was noticeably thinner, not to mention paler, with dark circles under her eyes.

Even so, she was still just as beautiful as a year ago. Flashes of their night together rushed over him, and it took everything Jake had to push them back. "Hello, Sylvia."

She smiled. "Hiya, Jake. Sorry about Connor. He's a wee bit protective these days."

Connor's voice came from behind Jake. "For good reason. You bloody fainted half an hour ago."

Concerned, Jake moved closer to Sylvia. "Are you okay?"

She waved a hand in dismissal. "I'll be fine. I just haven't had enough sleep or eaten as I should've done." She studied him a second and asked, "So why are you here?"

He glanced at Connor, and the man rolled his eyes. "Fine, I'll give you some privacy. I'll be upstairs if you need me, Mum."

Once they were alone, Jake stared at Sylvia again. Not liking the tension in the air, he decided to tease. "Five children, huh?"

Her lips twitched. "Aye, well, my late mate—er, husband—and I wanted a big family. We were young and rather industrious."

"So that's just another way to say you were busy between the sheets then?"

A blush crept over her cheeks and he relaxed a fraction. She'd blushed easily the year before, too, and it reminded him that this was the same dragonwoman he'd ravished that one night.

He walked closer and gestured toward the couch. "May I?"

"Of course. No need to be so formal."

As she sipped from her mug, her blush deepened.

She was no doubt remembering just how informal they'd been before.

He sat down and turned toward her. Jake itched to brush the hair off her face and finally touch her skin again. However, he kept his hands on his thighs and decided to finally answer her earlier question. "I'm here because you slipped out during the night, without so much as saying goodbye."

She set her mug down on the table next to the couch. "I thought it best."

He searched her face. "Why?"

She rearranged her blanket and turned more toward him. "Truthfully? I was ill—with something you couldn't catch, if you're worried—and the doctors didn't think I would live much longer. But I enjoyed our night, Jake, more than you'll ever know. However, I didn't want to drag you into my family drama. That would've been unfair. And so to protect you, I left."

She'd wanted to protect him? Even if he wished she would've talked with him instead of fleeing, he had to admit the dragonwoman was still as sweet and thoughtful as he remembered.

Oh, she'd tried to be bold last year, but the ruse had only worked so well.

Although he didn't like the fact she'd hidden something so huge from him.

He searched her eyes, wondering how bad her illness was. He finally reached out a finger to lightly brush her cheek. "Are you still ill?"

She leaned into his touch a second before backing

away. "No. Something finally cured me. I'm no longer terminally ill, just exhausted from something else. I'll be right as rain soon enough, as long as I get some sleep and remember to eat."

For some reason, he wanted to help take care of her. It was stupid, given he'd known her a day, but the feeling was still there.

Not wanting to dwell on how fanciful his thoughts were becoming, he changed the subject. "I looked for you at the expo again this year, but to no avail. My baking partner wasn't anywhere near as charming as you either. He could've been my grandfather, and since he forgot his glasses, he kept confusing the salt and sugar."

She smiled. "I wanted to go, but I couldn't."

He searched her eyes. "Why not?"

As she bit her lower lip, he waited. She finally murmured, "I just couldn't."

He was about to push when a baby's cry sounded from upstairs. Sylvia closed her eyes briefly and then tried to stand up. However, she swayed and Jake instantly stood to catch her. She leaned against him and looked up into his eyes. Her pupils flashed a few times, but it didn't bother him. He'd seen her dragon in full control before.

He finally tucked a section of her hair behind her ear and his fingers lingered on her jaw.

As they stared at one another, electricity sparked

between them, and he felt the same pull he had a year ago.

His eyes moved to her lips, and she licked the lower one. Fuck, he wanted to kiss her.

But the baby's wail grew louder and Connor's voice boomed down the stairs. "Mum, we can't get her quiet."

It was as if cold water sloshed over her, and Sylvia pulled away from Jake. She shouted back, "Bring her downstairs."

"Are you sure?" Connor bellowed.

"Aye. Fetch your sister."

He frowned. Sylvia had a baby too?

Sylvia sat back on the couch and rearranged the blanket over her lap. He was about to ask what was going on when Connor entered the room with a hiccupping, red-faced baby cradled against his chest, facing forward.

A baby with red hair a fraction lighter than his, and while much smaller, the nose was the same shape as his as well.

Sylvia said, "This is Sophie Rose. She's your daughter, Jake. Well, more correctly, our daughter."

Even with the evidence before him, he blinked, trying to process her words. "My…daughter?"

Connor walked over and handed the babe to Sylvia. Jake watched as she cuddled the fussy baby, which only made her cry louder.

Never taking her gaze from the child, Sylvia

replied, "Aye. If you want to leave now, I understand. But I thought you should know."

As he stared at the tiny thing in Sylvia's arms, he tried to process the fact he had a child.

A daughter.

And as she continued to cry and fuss, Sylvia's eyes were wet, looking about ready to cry herself. In that moment, his shock faded. He instantly knew why she looked so tired, and he held out his arms. "Let me hold her."

Sylvia hesitated a beat before she handed her over, and Jake cradled the baby in his arms. As he rocked her—just like he'd done with his nieces and nephews when they were younger—he hummed a lullaby.

She soon quieted and stared at him with her big eyes, mostly still baby blue with flecks of brown.

Given how much she resembled him, she'd probably end up with hazel eyes too.

"Sophie," he whispered, and she snuggled against his chest.

It was almost as if she knew he was her dad.

He'd never thought he'd be a father, but as the tiny angel fell asleep in his arms, Jake wanted to do everything to protect her.

His daughter.

When he could finally tear his gaze away from his child, he looked at Sylvia. And she promptly burst into tears.

SYLVIA KNEW she was being silly. But the sight of Jake holding Sophie, rocking her and humming to her, released a flood of emotion.

She'd wondered for months what it'd be like to see him with their daughter in his arms, staring at her with love.

And to have him there, in her cottage, doing exactly that made her realize how much she'd been struggling to be both mother and father to her bairn.

Not to mention the way Sophie instantly fell asleep in Jake's arms made Sylvia think their daughter had sorely wanted to meet her father too.

Her inner dragon said softly, *He's here now. And given how fiercely he's holding her, I don't think he's going to run away.*

She wiped away her tears just as Jake sat beside her slowly so as to not wake Sophie. He kept his voice low as he said, "I wish I'd known."

Nodding, she replied, "Aye, I know. But I didn't have any way to find you." She searched his gaze and then asked, "But you believe me that she's yours?"

He gently adjusted Sophie into the crook of one arm and then raised his free hand to brush away Sylvia's lingering tears, his warm touch helping to calm her down further.

He smiled. "She looks just like me, so it's kind of hard to ignore." He lowered his hand and gently took hers. Sylvia instantly wrapped her fingers around his, his strength somehow helping her to tame her emotions. "I'm still kind of surprised, though, and I'm sure it's going to take a while to wear off completely. But she's how old now?"

"Three months."

"Yep, that makes me the dad. Unless you go around seducing red-haired men on a regular basis?"

She actually laughed. "Of course not. To be honest, I'm still surprised I ended up in bed with you, Jake."

"Why's that?"

"Aye, well…you were my first in a long, long while."

"How long?"

Her cheeks heated, but she still answered, "Eleven years."

His eyes widened a second before he grinned. "Well, it's like riding a bike, right? You must've been really good at it before."

And now her whole face burned. She murmured, "I do have five older children."

He chuckled quietly. The simple act showed her how he was trying not to wake the bairn, and it did something to her heart.

Of all the scenarios she'd imagined of how this would play out, Jake sitting with Sophie in his arms and laughing with her had been toward the bottom of the list.

Her inner dragon spoke up. *Why? He drove all the way up just to see you. He's clearly interested.*

Or was *interested.*

Her beast sighed. *Don't dismiss him so easily.*

Jake tilted his head a fraction. "What did your dragon say?"

She raised her brows. "You're always going to ask me that, aren't you?"

He grinned. "Yep. I rather like your dragon."

Her beast stood tall inside her mind and all but preened at the praise.

Sylvia said to Jake, "She's just being your champion."

"Champion for what?"

"For why you're still here."

He frowned. "Well, I have permission to stay for a while, thanks to my cousin. So I'd like to get to know both you and my daughter, if you'll let me."

Her heart fluttered, but Sylvia did her best to contain it. After a week of changing nappies, cleaning up vomit, and getting frequent headaches from Sophie's crying, he might not be quite so enthusiastic about it all. She loved her daughter, but she was easily the fussiest of any of her brood.

Still, she owed him the benefit of the doubt. "I'd like you to stay. Although I'm going to be honest, Jake. I'm not quite the female you met back in Glasgow."

He raised an eyebrow. "How so?"

Leave it to her to have to list out her faults. But there was more at stake than merely Sylvia dating a handsome male. Sophie's entire future with her father depended on how Sylvia handled things.

If there was to be any sort of friendly relationship between them for their daughter's sake, it was going to have to be more honest and upfront than either of them probably liked.

Part of her longed for the playfulness and flirting from their one magical day a year ago. However, Sylvia didn't expect there to be any actual romantic relationship. There were far too many reasons it wouldn't work—distance, their respective lives, and that didn't even touch upon how emotionally fragile she was both due to her daughter's recent birth and the fact she still missed her late mate after all these years.

No, if Jake merely came to see his daughter occasionally, she'd count that as a win.

Her beast growled. *Stop dismissing him before he's even started.*

Ignoring her dragon, she answered Jake, "I'm not as straightforward as I was the day we met. I'm rather shy, and a mother of six, and also not very outgoing. I was trying my best to be more spontaneous when I was in Glasgow, but it took all my energy to do that for a day. It's simply not who I am."

Jake squeezed her hand in his, and Sylvia did her best to ignore the butterflies in her stomach at his firm, warm touch. He answered, "You're not acting that much different right now compared to last year. The only difference is that I have a baby in my arms and I'm holding back on kissing you until you feel better."

She raised her brows. "You want to kiss me?"

He released her hand and traced her bottom lip with his thumb. "More than anything. You're still beautiful, Sylvia. And sweet." He traced her cheek. "You blush more than anyone I know, which is charming." He took her chin in his hands. "At least give me the two weeks the DDA granted me to stay on Lochguard so I can both get to know you and Sophie." He stroked the soft underside of her chin. "Tell me I can."

As his hazel eyes stared into hers, Sylvia's exhaustion and frustration melted away.

If it was just her, it would be so easy to fall under Jake's charm. To grow addicted to him, his touch, the way he made her feel beautiful, and even the way he made her smile.

And yet, it wasn't just her.

Sylvia's gaze settled on Sophie's sleeping face. She murmured, "You can stay for Sophie." She finally met his eyes again. "But I'm not sure you'll have time for much else."

He leaned forward a fraction—as much as he could without jostling their daughter—and whispered, "I'm very, very good at time management, my dragon lady. I will most definitely stay for Sophie, but I'm also going to stay for you."

At the set of his jaw and the heat in his eyes, she swallowed.

Jake Swift might be human, but he had the determination—and probably stubbornness, judging from his words—of a dragon-shifter.

Part of her was thrilled.

However, the other part was worried. If she grew attached, she'd probably fall into another state of depression again when he left.

Because of course he would leave eventually. His life was back in America.

So the best thing was to protect her heart as much as she could. That way, once Jake was gone, she'd be able to take care of her daughter as she should.

Sylvia refused to fail Sophie in the way she'd failed her other five children, back when Arthur had died.

The hard part would be controlling her dragon.

Her beast huffed. *Speak for yourself. I want him. You do too. You'll realize that soon enough.*

What I want doesn't matter, dragon. Sophie means everything. Not to mention Cat will have her bairn soon and will need my help too. I won't let my children down this time.

Cat was Sylvia's eldest daughter, who was roughly eight months pregnant and on bedrest. The entire clan teased them about mother and daughter having children within months of each other.

Thankfully her beast fell silent and didn't argue further.

Sylvia cleared her throat and stood, her feet steadier this time around. She went to the doorway. "Connor, come down here." She then turned to Jake. "You can stay with Sophie and Connor whilst I make some lunch. You aren't allergic to anything, are you?"

He shook his head. However, just as Jake opened his mouth, her eldest son appeared, cutting him off. She gestured toward Jake and Sophie before the human could reply. "Play nice and just watch them."

Before Jake or Connor could say anything, Sylvia fled to the kitchen.

Aye, she fled. Because she needed time to think, to regain her strength, and figure out how to be around Jake for two weeks and not kiss him again.

Chapter Four

J ake felt the dragonman's eyes on him, but he ignored Connor to stare at his daughter and took her tiny hand in his.

He knew why Sylvia had insisted the boy watch them. Jake was, after all, still a virtual stranger.

What concerned him more was how Sylvia had fled. Not to mention the way she'd dismissed him having enough time for both Sylvia and Sophie.

True, they had a daughter together, but that didn't necessarily equate a happily ever after. Unplanned pregnancies happened all the time.

But Jake wanted more than that. Or at least the chance for more. Not only because he wanted to be near his child, but he had a feeling he'd never get Sylvia out of his head, no matter how much time had passed.

Hell, it'd been a year and he still dreamed of

their night together on a regular basis. Finding out he had a child with the beautiful woman of his dreams only made him want to try all the harder.

Jake was good at plans. It was what had made him the successful restauranteur he was. He'd just need to think of how to approach this situation. While not the same as figuring out locations, staff, menus, and the like, he would think of something. He just needed to get to know Sylvia a little better first.

Well, Sylvia and all six of her children, too, since they were obviously a close-knit family and a packaged deal.

Connor's voice—softer this time, no doubt for Sophie's sake—stated, "So you're staying, aye?"

He knew dragon-shifters had better senses, especially hearing and sight, than humans. Still, he finally met Connor's gaze and raised his brows. "Were you supposed to be eavesdropping?"

The young man sat up taller. "When it concerns my mum, of course I do."

Sensing the dragonman liked being direct instead of beating around the bush, he asked, "How old are you?"

The dragonman bristled, as if people always dismissed him because of his youth. "Why does that matter?"

Jake merely shrugged the shoulder of his free arm. "Call me crazy, but I thought it'd be nice to get to know my daughter's siblings a little better."

Connor grunted. "You abandoned my mum. Don't expect me to be nice to you."

He sighed. "I didn't know that I'd abandoned her. And then something happened in my family that I had to help with, or I would've come to Scotland sooner. If nothing else, I think we both care for our families, right?"

Connor didn't soften at all. "My family means everything to me. And anyone that hurts them, well, aye, they're going to have to deal with me."

Jake knew Connor was serious, and yet it took everything he had not to smile. The dragonman was so young and yet trying so hard. "Twenty-three? Am I close?"

His pupils flashed. "I just turned twenty-five. More than old enough to help my family."

Jake wondered if everyone underestimated Connor because of his age. "Of course it is."

The words seemed to stroke the younger man's ego a little. He studied Jake a few beats before saying softly, "Mum's had a hard time of it. Don't hurt her. I don't know if she can take it."

He frowned at Connor's words, but a doorway opened and voices filled the hallway before Jake could say anything else. Within seconds, Ian MacAllister and two more dark-haired young people stood in the living room.

As the three new arrivals frowned down at him,

his lips twitched. "Let me guess—two more of my daughter's five siblings? Where's the last one?"

Ian and the still-unnamed man growled, but the only young woman rolled her eyes and pushed past them. "Ignore my testosterone-filled brothers. I'm Emma, the fourth youngest. The eldest, my sister Cat, is on bedrest. She's about to pop out her bairn any second, so it doesn't surprise me she can't charge over here like she'd want to."

Jake blinked. "Sylvia's daughter is about to have a baby?"

Emma shrugged. "Strange, isn't it? Aunt and niece will be months apart. It was the talk of the clan until you showed up. Everyone is going to want to meet you now, so be prepared for some inventive reasons for them to just drop by, aye?"

He muttered, "More than enough have already gawked."

Emma snorted. "They're not who you have to worry about."

Jake glanced at each of the four siblings in the room. "Why? Is it the four of you I have to worry about?"

The only man he didn't know the name of—the one who looked to be the youngest—smirked. "No, that would be Finn."

The name rang a bell. He'd seen it often enough in his paperwork. "The clan leader."

The man opened his mouth, but Emma beat him

to it. "Haud yer wheesht, Jamie. Finn gave me the message, probably because he knew I wouldn't kick Jake's arse before he even had a chance." She faced Jake again. "Aye, Finn's the clan leader. He sent us here to help Mum with Sophie so you can chat with him." She put out her arms. "I can take her."

Jake instinctively leaned away and held his daughter closer. "I just met her."

Emma's gaze softened a fraction. "Aye, I know. But she'll be here when you return, I promise." His gaze traveled to the door Sylvia had exited. As if reading his thoughts, Emma added, "We'll look after her too."

Sophie squirmed a second in his arms, drawing his attention. Just as she snuggled more against his chest, strong emotion flooded him.

Was it possible to love someone so quickly?

He traced her soft cheek, smoothed down her flyaway hair nearly the same color as his own, and leaned down to kiss her forehead. He murmured, "I'll be back as soon as I can, Sophie girl. Be good for your mom, okay?"

Sophie continued to snore softly.

God, he didn't want to leave his daughter so soon. And yet if he pissed off the clan leader, he might not get the chance to know her at all.

Standing carefully so as not to wake her, he held the slight, warm weight of his daughter another few beats before gingerly passing Sophie to her sister.

Thankfully Sophie stayed asleep and Emma smiled at him. "Aye, well, know that at least I like you." She motioned toward her brothers. "If that lot gives you trouble, just say the word and I'll teach them a lesson."

Jamie muttered something, but Jake ignored him to touch Sophie's cheek one last time before dropping his arm. "I'll be back as soon as I can. Although I hope someone can guide me, or it's going to take me a hell of a long time to find my way around, knocking on doors until I get to the right one."

Ian snorted. "Come on. I'm the least likely to challenge you the entire way. Let's go before Jamie feels the need to prove how strong he is again."

Jamie frowned as his cheeks colored slightly.

Jake knew what it was like to be the little brother, and it wasn't always easy. Taking a shot, he asked, "You're the youngest, aren't you?"

The dragonman blinked. "Aye."

"So am I." He smiled. "Maybe we can help each other? One youngest sibling to another?"

Jamie stared a second and said, "Um, aye?"

He nodded and slapped the dragonman's shoulder. "Then I'll see you later."

Ian led the way and Jake followed, doing his best to gather his thoughts. He had a feeling it was going to take everything he had to face the clan leader and live to tell the tale. Even if Finn had granted Jake permission to visit Lochguard, he could order him to leave at any moment.

Jake just needed to ensure that didn't happen.

Sylvia was still fixing sandwiches in the kitchen when her middle daughter walked in. Since Emma was the bluntest of all her children, it should no longer surprise her what came out of the female's mouth. However, when she asked, "Is he going to be our stepdad?" Sylvia froze.

Clearing her throat, she continued cutting the sandwich in front of her. "No."

Emma swiped a sliced tomato and said, "I like him. He didn't want to let Sophie out of his sight. Even though he's human, he seems like a good male. Sexy, too, even if he's a wee bit old for me. His accent just adds to his appeal as well, don't you think?"

Knowing that if she didn't put this to rest now, Emma would keep prodding until Sylvia either threw her hands up in exasperation or, on rare occasions, lost her temper. Turning to face her daughter, she stated, "I want him to know Sophie, aye, of course I do. But that's it. Don't meddle, Emma."

Her daughter swallowed her bite of tomato before replying, "I only meddle when absolutely necessary." Sylvia raised an eyebrow and Emma sighed. Her daughter added, "Okay, so sometimes I do it because I'm trying to help people see what's right in front of them. But it's worked out well a few times, aye? That should make up for all my failures."

Even though Sylvia had eaten a snack and fortified herself with plenty of tea, meaning she wasn't going to faint anytime soon, she still nearly massaged her temples. Emma was clever, too much so for her twenty-three years, and trying to argue with her could last a long time.

So she decided blunt honesty was the best route. "Sophie, and soon Cat, need me. I may no longer be ill or afraid of dying, but raising a child as a single parent is exhausting. I don't have the energy for more than the six of you and my soon-to-be grandchild."

Emma's voice turned serious as she said, "Us older children can take care of ourselves. Besides, you're lonely, Mum. Dad died twelve years ago. It's okay to find and care for someone else."

She quickly pushed aside the pang she always felt when her children mentioned their father. "And that only reinforces my point about keeping my distance. I love you, Emma, but I'm not like you when it comes to flirting with one male and then another. I get attached rather easily, and when something is torn away from me, it devastates me. You were old enough to remember how I couldn't get out of bed for weeks once your father died. Even if it's not death and would merely be a male leaving, I can't risk another spell, not with Sophie to think of. Recognizing my faults is all I can do in this situation, and make the best of it."

Emma said softly, "But you're also the mother who says we shouldn't be too afraid to try something new, to fight against expectations to be happy. I may not deal with males in the same way as you, but you have no idea the amount of shite I have to put up with in my line of work. Females aren't supposed to be good at hacking, or coding, or with computers in general. At first, it hurt me that everyone dismissed me because of my age and gender. But you know what? In the end, it was worth all the crap I endured to do something that I enjoy, something that helps the clan." She bit her lip—a sign her daughter was gathering her thoughts—and then added, "What I'm trying to say is that sometimes you have to risk a little to get what you want. And that is something I learned from you and Dad. I only hope you remember it for yourself."

Before she could reply, Emma walked out of the kitchen, leaving Sylvia to ponder her daughter's words.

On the one hand, she was proud of how Emma had grown up. Aye, she was a massive gossip and flirt, but when it really counted, her daughter knew what mattered.

And yet, Emma's words made Sylvia doubt herself a wee bit.

Should she risk a little to see if Jake could be

more than merely a father to Sophie? Or should she play it safe to ensure she didn't fail her children again when she faced heartbreak?

If she faced heartbreak.

Her dragon was never the chattiest of beasts, but she finally spoke up. *I think you know the answer already. You took a risk last year and had the best day in over a decade.*

Aye, but that was for a day, not weeks or months, let alone forever.

Then don't think of forever. Take it as it goes because Emma's right—you're lonely. And tired. And frustrated. At least give the human a chance to know us better.

Oh, how she wanted to. And yet, Sylvia didn't do half-measures. At least she'd never done so to date.

Could she really take it easy and just have fun with Jake and let things develop as they did?

Her dragon said, *Remember Gregor? He lost his mate and was determined to shut everyone out. Now he's mated for a second time and has a son. If he could risk it, why can't we?*

She and Dr. Gregor Innes had been friends in school, were around the same age, and both had endured the loss of their mates in rather tragic circumstances. His from complications with pregnancy and Sylvia from dragon hunters capturing and draining Arthur of blood.

Too bad Gregor now lived with Clan Stonefire down in England with his mate and son. Maybe talking with him would've helped.

Her dragon said softly, *I think you already know what you want but are afraid to admit it. Aye?*

The thing with inner beasts is that they knew a person better than anyone else.

And her dragon was right—if given the choice, she'd like more time with Jake. To laugh, to smile, to revel in the heat of a male body against hers.

To feel desired and special, to be more than just a mother, if only for a few moments.

Her dragon spoke up. *Then give him a chance. You don't have to plan the next five years, just the next two weeks. All you have to do is not fall in love with him right away.*

As if it were that easy. Sylvia had fallen in love with Arthur after a week of dating.

Still, she'd been sixteen back then, and now she was forty-four. Surely she could practice a bit more restraint.

She said to her beast, *I'll not shut him out completely, but that's all I can promise for now.*

Good. At least that's a start.

Smiling to herself, Sylvia assembled the sandwiches and went into the living room, only to find Emma, Jamie, Connor, and a sleeping Sophie, but no sign of Jake. "Where'd he go?"

Jamie plucked a sandwich from the plate and answered, "To see Finn."

Her first instinct was to go help Jake. He was human, not dragon-shifter, and despite Finn's usual jolly demeanor, he could be serious and stern when it came to his clan.

But then she realized Jake needed to handle Finn on his own. Because if he couldn't handle a clan leader, then he would never be able to live with a dragon clan.

Not that she was hoping he would. But she wouldn't completely dismiss anything going forward.

That would be the new Sylvia—one who didn't obsess over every detail and how it could go horribly wrong.

No, she was going to try and relax a little—not a lot, but a wee bit—and see how the cards fell.

Chapter Five

J ake entered the clan leader's office. However, before either of them could say a word, a tiny golden dragon sleeping next to Finn's desk stretched and settled down again. Nothing he'd ever read said young children could shift. He blurted, "Is that normal? Will my daughter be in her dragon form when I get back?"

Finn snorted, garnering Jake's attention. "No, my daughter Freya is special. Most dragons don't start shifting until they're six or seven years old." Finn waved to the chairs in front of his desk. "Sit down."

He complied, and the blond-haired dragon leader merely stared at him. Even though the man was a dragon-shifter, he was still younger than Jake. And while Jake may not have strength and super senses on his side, he knew how to stare and wait for someone to finally say what they needed to say.

Only then could Jake think of his next steps.

Leaning back in his chair, he tried his best to relax. Finn finally shook his head. "I must admit it's nice to have an older male, one who isn't out to prove he's worthy to anyone who dares him."

Jake smiled. "I'm guessing what I saw among Sylvia's sons is just a glimpse of all the young guys here."

"Aye, to a degree." Finn paused a second, his pupils flashing to slits and back to round again before adding, "I let you meet Sylvia first instead of with me so you could find out the truth. You've met Sophie now, aye?" Jake nodded. "So what do you plan to do now?"

Jake replied, "My paperwork grants me at least two weeks on Lochguard, with your continued permission, of course. I'd like to get to know both Sylvia and Sophie. Even if I can't stay longer, I'll come back to see my daughter again. I'm not going to abandon her, if that's what you're asking."

Finn steepled his fingers in front of him. "You accept her as yours so easily and now vow to be a part of her life. Why?"

He didn't miss a beat. "Family is important to me. And one look tells you Sophie is my daughter. So I want to make sure she knows her dad loves her."

"And what about Sylvia?"

Damn, Finn was direct, wasn't he? Jake knew exactly what he wanted with Sophie, but Sylvia was a lot more difficult. He decided to be honest. "That depends a lot on what Sylvia wants."

"So finding out you have a secret child doesn't make you want to run for the hills?"

"Of course not."

"Hmm." Jake debated whether he should say something else when Finn continued, "As long as Sylvia doesn't say otherwise, you can stay. For the two weeks, at least. If it reaches a point beyond that, we'll talk again. It seems that cousin of yours has a way with both Departments of Dragon Affairs in America and the UK. I'm impressed."

It didn't surprise Jake that Finn knew Ashley was his cousin, and not just because of the name. He had a feeling the clan leader had researched Jake before letting him come to Lochguard. "Ashley is one of the smartest people I know. Give her a chance, and she could probably form trans-Atlantic alliances without breaking a sweat."

Finn grinned. "That could be useful." He sobered. "But for now, my main concern is you. There is a cottage for you to use for the duration of your stay. It'll be between you and Sylvia as to if she and Sophie want to temporarily stay there, or if she wants to keep separate residences, or if you want to ask her kids to stay there for a bit so you can move into Sylvia's place to better help care for your daughter. Regardless, I'd suggest some time away from her older children. The males, especially, can be protective."

"Her kids are a huge part of her life, though. I think getting to know them is important."

"Aye, they are. But methinks you want to spend some time alone with Sylvia as well, unless the one night was enough?"

Apparently Finn knew more details than he'd thought. True, he'd have to have had sex at least once with Sylvia to get her pregnant, but had Sylvia told Finn all about their one night?

Regardless, he refused to comment on his night with Sylvia since it was between them, and he sure as hell wouldn't talk about it with the clan leader before the dragonwoman herself.

When Jake didn't answer, Finn snorted. "You'll soon learn that we're not shy about many things here—nudity, teasing people about sex, and more. Just wait until you meet her father-in-law. There are some tales there."

He blinked. "Excuse me?"

Finn waved a hand. "I'm sure you'll hear about Archie MacAllister soon enough. But sort out the living arrangements with Sylvia straight away. You and I will have another chat in a few days to see how things are going."

He frowned. "If you think I'm going to reveal all the inner workings of my private life, you'll be waiting a long time."

Finn snorted. "Calm yourself down, Yank. I check in with visitors regularly, regardless of who they are." The dragonman leaned forward a little. "I've dealt with bombs, and drugs, and all sorts of threats before. Trust me, you'll be easy for a change."

Jake thought of how to respond to that when something butted against his leg. He looked down to see the baby golden dragon looking up at him with big eyes.

Unsure of what to do, he lightly patted her on the head. Finn said, "Scratch behind her ears and she'll love you forever."

He found the small strip of exposed skin behind the ear—the one place without scales—and gently scratched. Freya hummed and closed her eyes, and Jake couldn't help but smile.

Finn sighed. "And she's won you over too. I swear, my own daughter will try to take over the clan from me by the time she's a teenager."

Jake could tell the words were said with love, though.

A question came into his mind. "Do all dragons liked to be scratched behind their ears?"

"Aye."

Suddenly, he wanted to see what Sylvia looked like as a dragon. He'd been so consumed with finding her and then digesting the news about his daughter that he'd forgotten how she was a dragon-shifter and not just another human.

Of course if he wanted to ask her that, he first needed to get his living situation figured out. Only then could he start thinking of how to help with Sophie and somehow spend some time alone with Sylvia too.

Finn called his daughter over, and she slowly waddled to him. Once she was in his lap, Finn said, "Go before Freya decides she wants you to stay longer." Jake stood, and Finn added, "Oh, and if it comes to needing a babysitter, my aunt Lorna Anderson is always happy to help. I know Sylvia has her kids, too, but I think everyone may need one night off in the near future."

He nodded, tucked away that piece of information, murmured his goodbye, and headed back toward Sylvia's house.

Now he needed to figure out his first step—living arrangements. And quickly. Which meant avoiding his daughter's adorableness long enough to have a serious conversation with Sylvia to lay out the beginnings of their relationship on Lochguard.

Jake knew which one he rooted for—he wanted to be around for everything. However, it would ultimately be Sylvia's choice. She'd seemed a little shyer and more hesitant than their first meeting in Glasgow.

But that was no matter. Until he'd given his all toward proving he could care for Sophie and that he at least wanted a chance with Sylvia, he'd do whatever it took.

He only hoped Sylvia didn't dismiss him before he even started.

Sylvia had learned long ago with her first child that whenever her bairn slept, she napped at the same time if she could, especially in the early months.

And since Sophie hadn't slept much over the past two days, Sylvia hadn't either. So when her children had offered to watch the sleeping Sophie while Jake talked with Finn, Sylvia had barely made it to her bed without stumbling. The second her head hit the pillow, she passed out.

By the time she woke up to shouts and laughter, the sun had set and been replaced by darkening twilight sky. A glance at the clock told her it was past seven, meaning she'd slept for nearly six hours.

Her first instinct was to look at the crib in her room to see if her offspring had brought Sophie in, but it was empty.

Sophie must still be with her siblings. However, Sophie hadn't yet mastered the art of sleeping half the day away—she still ate rather frequently—which meant her children must've used the frozen breast milk she kept for emergencies.

Although thinking of that made her realize she needed to find her daughter soon or she was going to burst.

Slowly she went into the hall and headed for the stairs, the shouts and laughter getting clearer.

It rather sounded like her older children were taunting one another. She even thought she heard Cat's voice.

Then Jake's clear voice rang out. "Now you have to draw ten cards, Connor. Unless you can pile on."

She frowned, and as she reached the entryway to the living room, Sylvia hovered to take in the scene.

All five of her grown children, plus Cat's mate Lachlan, were playing some sort of color-coded card game around the coffee table. She scanned for Sophie and finally saw her in her father's arm, gnawing on one of her plastic ring toys.

It was Cat who noticed her first. She grinned and said, "You're finally awake, Mum."

She frowned. "Aren't you supposed to be home on bedrest?"

Cat rolled her eyes. "Lachlan only let me come if he could push me in a wheelchair. The rest of the time I've been sitting here, unless I have to pee, which is all the time. I won't miss the wee one kicking my bladder at all."

Her daughter's mate nodded in greeting— Lachlan was more the silent, watchful type—and then she caught Jake's eyes. He spoke before she could say anything. "We didn't wake you, did we? If I'd known how much of a sore loser Connor was, I would've thought of something else to do."

Connor growled. "I'm not a sore loser. But when all of you gang up on me so that I end up with twenty bloody cards in my hand, I'm allowed to be irritated."

Emma punched his shoulder lightly. "You're the oldest sibling in the house now, which means we're *supposed* to irritate you."

Cat chuckled and Sylvia resisted a sigh. She asked, "What're you playing?"

Jake answered, "A card game called Uno. We're playing with Swift family rules, which means you can be evil and maniacal and force someone to easily end up with twenty cards in their hands, maybe even forty, if you play with multiple decks and team up with everyone."

She moved closer. "It definitely sounds like something the MacAllister family would enjoy."

He grinned and patted the empty spot next to him. "I can teach you how to play, if you want."

She nearly shouted yes. But then Sophie saw her, made some noises that would soon turn into crying, and her breasts ached. "I need to feed Sophie first. Maybe after?"

Holding out her arms, she waited. Jake stood and slowly placed their daughter in her arms. Sylvia smiled at him a beat longer than was probably necessary before saying, "I'll be back soon."

When he lightly touched her arm, she resisted shivering at his warm fingers. He murmured, "Can I come with you?"

She easily noticed the longing in his eyes, as if he wanted to make up for lost time with his daughter. Normally, Sylvia didn't think twice about feeding her daughter in her own house. And yet, doing so in front of Jake would make her self-conscious.

Her dragon sighed. *Stop worrying. It's not like he's going to ravish you whilst nursing Sophie.*

Clearing her throat, Sylvia nodded. "I have a rocking chair I like to use in my bedroom."

He smiled, and as she turned, he placed a hand on the small of her back, his touch calming and yet a wee bit possessive.

It was Connor's voice who snapped Sylvia back to the present, where all her children sat watching her and Jake. "I'll fix dinner in the meantime."

Cat snorted. "Anything to avoid losing again."

Connor's pupils flashed. "I wasn't losing, but trying to survive an all-out attack. There's a difference."

Cat raised an eyebrow. "Sounds like losing to me."

As the pair argued, Sylvia murmured to Jake, "Come on. If we wait for them to finish, it could end up being morning before you know it."

He chuckled but moved along with her up the stairs. "Even from what small amount of time I've spent with them, it's easy to see they all love each other."

She glanced at him. "They do. And it was nice of you to play cards with them."

His hand moved to the side of her waist and squeezed. "You needed to sleep and I needed to face the firing squad."

She frowned. "Please tell me they aren't threatening you still."

"No, no, nothing like that. Well, mostly. It was just a lot of questions about what I do, where I live, the usual. Your eldest daughter is quite persistent when she wants to be."

Sylvia wondered if her children now knew more about Jake than she did. A thread of jealousy shot through her, but she pushed it away. She was merely going to have to find time to spend with him. Preferably alone. "Aye, she is. Cat had to grow up faster than she should have when my late mate died. But she has Lachlan now. He's relaxed her quite a bit and takes care of her, even when she doesn't think she needs it. He's human too, you know."

"Yeah, he mentioned it. Although he doesn't talk a whole lot."

She raised her brows. "Do you think anyone can really get a word in around my children?"

He grinned. "It can be done, and I managed

pretty well. American confidence really does come in handy with your family, I think."

"American cockiness, you mean?"

He placed a hand over his heart in mock hurt. "You wound me, madam. Deeply."

She laughed and gently pushed against his side. "You're a hardy lad. You'll be fine."

"I'm more than a lad." His gaze turned heated and his voice husky as he added, "I'm all man for you."

Sylvia wanted to roll her eyes at his words, but instead, her heart thumped harder, and awareness made her lower belly ache as she remembered how very male he'd been during their night together.

At some point, they'd stopped walking and merely stared at one another. But then Sophie squirmed, and Sylvia tore her gaze away from Jake's. "Sorry, lassie. Let's get you fed. You must be hungry, aye?"

She entered her room and sat in the rocking chair. After she tugged up her shirt and ensured Sophie latched, she began her normal routine of humming to her daughter as she nursed. It had helped in the early days to keep her from fussing, and now it was almost a tradition.

Jake moved next to the rocking chair and gently brushed Sophie's head. "Tell me your favorite memory of her so far."

For a second, guilt flooded her body. Milestones

with children were precious, especially with the first ones. Sophie may be Sylvia's sixth child, but she was Jake's first.

Or so she thought.

Realizing she didn't know much about him, she blurted, "Do you have other children?"

He knelt so he could look into Sylvia's eyes. "No, just Sophie."

As he looked again at their daughter, Sylvia briefly wished Jake could be around always, to see everything yet to come.

But rather than focus on the future, she answered his question about the past. "I have two favorite memories, actually. The first was discovering she had nearly a full head of ginger hair at her birth. All my other children have dark hair, and it's like she wanted to be different, to stand out in the crowd." She smiled down at Sophie. "It's also why her middle name is Rose, because I remembered you creating the flowers for the cake during the competition. It's not much, but it was a small way to honor a memory of her dad."

Jake touched Sophie's hair again, as if it would help him imagine Sophie's birth. After a second, he asked softly, "And the other memory?"

The sight of his large hand delicately stroking Sophie's wee one did something to her heart. But she focused on answering, "She's started babbling in the last week or so. There's something charming about it, like she's trying to tell me everything and I can't understand it." She looked at Jake. "Did she babble for you whilst I was sleeping?"

He nodded. "Yes. Although I swear it's in a Scottish accent, as weird as that sounds."

She laughed. "Well, aye, she lives in Scotland, after all. To her, you probably sound strange. Not that she really understands us yet, but still."

For a second, they merely smiled at one another, and then Jake raised a hand to brush a section of hair off Sylvia's cheek. She nearly leaned into his touch, but he removed his fingers before she could do so.

Jake cleared his throat before saying, "Finn provided a cottage for me while I'm on Lochguard. I can stay there if it makes you more comfortable. Or…"

"Or what?"

He searched her gaze. "I can either stay here while your kids move in there, or you and Sophie can stay with me in the guest cottage. Just tell me where you want me to stay, Sylvia, and I'll do it."

Jake was being overly cautious with her.

And for some reason, she missed him from the year before, when he hadn't held back from telling her what he wanted.

Her dragon spoke up. *Then tell him to be honest and frank. He's not a mind reader.*

Her beast was right. With her late mate, she'd let

him be the forward one, always letting her know how he wanted her. Sylvia had been young, and a wee bit naïve, and glad to have someone offering the decisions for her.

But she was a grown female with six children. If she wanted something, she needed to say it and not wait around for it to happen.

So she replied, "I want you to stay here, with me and Sophie. The other four will grumble about being booted out for a bit, but they'll give us some space if I ask for it."

"Even the three boys?"

She smiled. "Aye, even them. They're protective, but I'm still their mum."

Jake lifted her free hand and kissed her fingers, his lips lingering a second before he murmured, "Then that's settled. I just need to get my things."

He rose to his feet, but she spoke before he took a step. "You can put your things here in my room, if you want."

He stared a second and then leaned down, taking her lips in a quick, rough kiss. His firm, soft lips made her want more of him, like she'd had before.

However, he soon pulled away, his face a few inches from hers before saying, "Be very sure of that, Sylvia. Because if I sleep in this room with you, I'm going to kiss you. A lot. And more, when you're ready."

Her dragon hummed. *Yes, I like that plan.*

Jake asked, "What did your dragon say?"

Wanting to keep the tradition from their first meeting, she said, "She likes your idea. Quite a bit."

He leaned over, lightly nibbled her earlobe, and whispered, "Good. Have I told you how much I like your dragon?"

She laughed, and Jake kissed her cheek before standing. His voice was husky as he stated, "I'll be back soon. Do you want me to tell your kids about the arrangements?"

She shook her head. "No, I should be the one to do it after I finish with Sophie."

He nodded, stared at her and Sophie for a few beats as if memorizing the scene, and then exited the room.

As Sylvia readjusted Sophie to her other breast, she murmured to her daughter, "Maybe since your daddy's coming to stay, you can try to sleep better for us, aye?"

Sophie was too busy eating to care, even if she could understand her question.

Sylvia hummed again. Both out of habit and because she was eager for Sophie to finish so she could tell her children of the temporary plans.

More than Jake staying around to better know his daughter, Sylvia wanted more than the human's kisses. Maybe it wouldn't happen tonight, but him moving in—albeit temporarily—meant they could know each other better.

And maybe, just maybe, they'd find some sort of pathway where they could be together, even if it seemed impossible in the present.

No. One day at a time—that was her new motto.

And Sylvia could tell she was going to have a devil of a time trying to stick to it.

Chapter Six

J ake had grabbed his stuff from the rental car, returned to Sylvia's place, and was promptly marched into the dining room by Emma and Jamie.

Apparently Connor had finished making dinner and they were all sitting down together, no matter what.

Sylvia murmured that they knew about the temporary living arrangements and would leave after the meal.

At least they'd let him sit next to her and not tried to place him between two of the sons. Emma sat across from him, her older sister, Cat, next to her, and Connor was on Jake's other side.

Although once everything was dished out, Jake didn't have a chance to say a word before Emma blurted, "Are you two going to share a room too?"

Jake blinked and Sylvia sighed. His dragonwoman answered, "Are you ever going to learn to be respectable to guests at the dinner table?"

Emma grinned. "Why? That wouldn't be any fun."

Lachlan chuckled and looked at Jake as he said, "She asked me something about shagging her sister at the first family dinner. I think Emma wants to shock people, just because. Don't you, lass?"

Emma shrugged. "Why beat around the bush when it comes to family? Besides, it's not like Jake hasn't slept with Mum before. I would hope everyone here knows where babies come from because I'd rather not be related to idiots."

He noticed Sylvia's cheeks flush. Jake wasn't easily embarrassed himself, but he didn't like how Emma's words made Sylvia uncomfortable.

And if Emma wanted to be blunt and borderline scandalous? Well, so could he. Jake asked, "And what about you? Do you want us asking if there are any guys debauching you recently? Breaking beds? Secret rendezvous in Inverness with a human that you shouldn't see?"

Emma didn't bat an eyelash. "Cat and Lachlan are the ones who break beds, not me."

Cat growled. "Can we not share that with everyone, aye? It's not like it's happened recently. I can barely waddle, let alone do anything acrobatic."

Lachlan merely sighed.

However, Jake jumped back in. "I think you change the subject when you don't want to talk about yourself, Emma. Is there something you're hiding?"

The young dragonwoman sat up taller. "Of course not."

The youngest son, Jamie, snorted. "You're lying. You always sit or stand taller when doing it, Em."

Emma slumped forward a little. "I'm not important. Jake here is the one we should focus on, aye? He's the newcomer."

Jake smiled. "You're doing it again."

Sylvia frowned. "Just tell me your secret won't endanger your life, aye? You're full grown and have a right to your privacy, but not if it's going to kill you."

Emma murmured, "It's nothing that will kill me, Mum. I promise."

Sylvia nodded. "Aye, well then we'll leave it at that." Her words held a sort of dominance he hadn't heard before, and wondered if that was due to her being a dragon-shifter or a mother.

She turned toward him and asked, "Maybe you can tell us about your restaurants? I doubt even my children can turn that into something embarrassing or scandalous."

The corner of his mouth ticked up. "You just all but issued a challenge to them, Sylvia."

She glanced at each of her children in turn. "Not

if I guilt-trip them about how I fainted earlier today and need some calm to fully recover."

Half of her kids rolled their eyes, but they murmured how they'd be good.

Under the table, he placed a hand on her leg and squeezed. She met his gaze and grinned. "You have to use what you can with this lot. Remember that."

Cat shook her head. "Such loving words, Mum."

Sylvia snorted. "Oh, rubbish, Cat. You used the same tactics with your siblings growing up."

Lachlan wrapped an arm around Cat's shoulders and nodded. "I love you, but she's right, lass. It's advice you gave me too."

Cat glared. "You're supposed to be on my side."

"I am, love. But the truth is more important, aye?"

She muttered, "Bloody stupid vow to honesty," before shoving some potatoes into her mouth.

Jake answered Sylvia's question, saying, "I have three restaurants in the San Francisco area."

Connor perked up. "That's quite the achievement for your age, aye?"

He shrugged. "It was a dream of mine, and I've spent more than twenty years making it happen." He smiled. "And it's not as if forty-three is a toddler, barely learning to walk."

Connor replied, "Well, I mostly run Mum's restaurant now. And I'm only twenty-five."

Jake bit back a smile at the boy's bragging. "You'll

have to show me around soon, then. I'm curious to see if a dragon-shifter's place is really that different from a human one or not."

Sylvia answered, "Mostly just that the portion sizes are bigger. Or, rather, I should say they're American-sized."

He raised his brows. "Have you been to the US?"

She shook her head. "No, but I've run my restaurant for more than twenty years and visited enough events to hear the talk."

He shrugged. "There's nothing better than having enough to take home in a doggy bag and eat it the next day. Then the meal lasts two days."

Sylvia said, "Maybe so, but it's nice to have a fresh meal each day, aye?"

Jamie spoke up. "Not that it matters in this house. Connor, Ian, and I eat everything we can find. Emma, too, although she tries to hide it."

Emma raised her brows. "I don't hide it. I just have to sneak it out before you lot get to it."

And most of the children started arguing again.

However, Sylvia placed her hand on top of his under the table and squeezed. He met her gaze and she murmured, "Thank you."

He leaned over and whispered, "For what?"

"For not getting angry at their antics, or frustrated, or any number of ways others might react."

Jake wondered if more people than not lost

patience with her kids. "I find it amusing. Besides, my nieces and nephews are just as bad, maybe even louder, if that's possible."

Or, rather, it was just the one nephew now.

Not that he was going to bring that up and ruin the evening.

He quickly murmured, "Although as entertaining as they are, when can we kick them out and be alone for a little while?"

Her pupils flashed to slits and back again before she replied, "Soon. They're finishing up dessert. And as long as you don't mind doing the dishes later, I can shoo them away for the night once they're done."

Her hand squeezed his again, and the touch made him think of what he wanted to do to his dragon lady when they were alone.

Especially if Sophie slept well in the night.

Not that he'd force her into anything, but every cell in his body itched to kiss her again. And maybe hold her close.

They'd had such little time together since his arrival, and it was high time to rectify it.

As soon as Cat finished her dessert, Lachlan declared they were leaving. Sylvia gave a few hints to her other children, and they grudgingly took the keys from Lachlan that Finn had given him, gathered their stuff, said their goodbyes, and one by one, left with their bags.

Once Jamie—the last to leave—was gone, he cupped Sylvia's cheek and murmured, "As much as I like your kids, I'm happy they're gone."

She smiled, her eyes flashing. "Me, too."

He leaned closer, until his lips were an inch from hers, and asked, "And what's your dragon saying now?"

Her hands lay on his chest and stroked up and down, sending heat throughout his body. "She's wondering why you haven't kissed us yet."

"Then let's not disappoint your dragon."

Jake closed the scant distance between them and took her lips in a slow, gentle kiss. He teased, nibbled, licked, and when she finally moaned and parted, he took advantage and entered her mouth.

Her heat, her taste, and even her small moan snapped something inside of him. He pressed her against him, her soft belly cushioning his cock, and put every bit of desire, and wanting, and sheer need he'd been bottling up into the kiss.

There was so much they still didn't know about each other, but in this moment, none of it mattered. Because if he didn't kiss her, and hold her, and revel in her warmth, he felt as if he might die.

When her nails dug into his back, he groaned. And then Sylvia took control of the kiss, exploring his mouth, battling his tongue, pressing more against him, as if they couldn't get close enough.

Fuck, he wanted her. All of her.

And yet he wondered if this was right. Maybe he should take it slow, get to know her better, prove he wanted more than sex with her.

Because he did. Even if there were a lot of unknowns, he'd never felt so right with another woman, desired someone so much, to the point he couldn't imagine never seeing or holding her again.

It was why he'd traveled halfway around the world just for the chance to talk with her.

With every iota of self-restraint he possessed, Jake broke the kiss and pressed his forehead to hers. Both of them breathed heavily, and he could see the desire and heat in Sylvia's eyes. Her pupils flashed a few times before she asked, "Why did you stop?"

"Between me showing up and you fainting, you've had quite the day and I didn't want to take advantage."

She stroked his jaw, and the light touch shot straight to his cock. "I've had a long nap, plenty to eat, and I can shift into a rather large dragon. If I didn't want this, you'd know."

He searched her gaze. "Are you sure, Sylvia? You're the sexiest woman I've ever met, and damn, I want you. But I can wait. I can tell you more about me, learn more about you, even spend more time with your kids, if that's what it takes. Because in the end, we might not know each other well, but my gut tells me you're worth it."

She smiled and kissed his jaw. "You just become better with time, aye? I sometimes wonder if I'm dreaming."

"I've had a lot of dreams of you over the last year, and trust me, this is so much better."

Her smile widened. "You're as charming as I remember."

"Only with you, not just anyone."

She ran her fingers through his hair and he leaned into the touch. "Sophie's asleep in the secondary crib we put in Cat's old room—it was in case her bairn came over after she was born. So my room is empty." She leaned more against him. "And did I mention our daughter is asleep?"

He gave her a quick, rough kiss before murmuring, "Then we'd best take advantage."

He swooped Sylvia off her feet and carried her up the stairs.

Jake hadn't planned on this so soon, but hell, Sylvia wanted it as much as he did.

And he wasn't about to deny his sexy dragon lady.

SYLVIA'S HEART thudded as Jake carried her up the stairs and into her bedroom.

Earlier, she'd thought about putting off sex until they'd talked more. Maybe learned his favorite food, or the name of his family members, or even just what he liked to do in his free time.

And yet, the tension hummed between them constantly. Attraction was what had brought them together in the first place, giving her the gift of Sophie, and eventually had resulted in Jake coming to find her.

She had a feeling they both needed this—sex, and kissing, and orgasms—before they could relax and think more of the future.

Her dragon spoke up. *Remember, you're not going to plan it all out this time, aye?*

I know. But it's hard. For now, I'm just trying to enjoy tonight without thinking of more.

Good. Have some fun. You deserve it.

Before she could reply, Jake laid her on the bed, covered her body with his, and all other thoughts fled her mind as he kissed her. This time, it was slow, gentle, and lazy, almost as if saying they had all the time in the world.

Clearly he'd never tried having sex with a young bairn in the house.

She pulled back and whispered, "Take off your clothes. Hurry, in case Sophie wakes up."

After one more quick kiss, he stripped his clothes off as she did the same.

Sylvia took in his broad shoulders, strong arms, and the dark ginger hair on his chest, leading down to his groin. His cock was hard and long, and just as thick as she remembered.

In a flash, any tiredness or worry about the future fled. Sylvia just wanted to feel a strong male above her, around her, inside her, making her forget everything else for a wee while.

Jake stroked his dick and turned toward his bags. When he pulled out a condom, Sylvia said, "Wait."

He gave her a puzzled look, and she added, "That's what got us into trouble last time. Human condoms and, er, dragon-shifters don't mix well. They're fairly useless with female dragons—they break down." She gestured toward her drawer, "But there should be some in there that will work."

Emma had told her she'd snuck some into her room. Thank goodness for her responsible daughter, even if Sylvia didn't want to be thinking of her until recently youngest daughter sleeping with however many males.

Jake took one of the dragon-approved condoms out and as he rolled it on, said, "Why didn't you say anything last time?"

"Er, well. My late mate was a dragon-shifter. And we were industrious, if you remember. Condoms were never really needed." Not to mention Arthur had eventually gotten a vasectomy, making them unnecessary altogether. "And whilst we're told about such things in our early teens, do you remember much from school twenty-odd years ago, about topics you never thought you'd need to know?"

Condom on, he crawled over her on the bed. "I'm not the best one to ask that question since I have a stellar memory." She opened her mouth, but he placed a finger over her lips. "But I don't care. For whatever reason, it worked out. Otherwise, we wouldn't have Sophie."

For all that Sylvia had thought she'd been done having children, she couldn't imagine her life without her ginger-haired daughter now.

And knowing that Jake didn't regret her, either, did something to her heart.

Focus on just tonight, Sylvia. She reached a hand up and threaded her fingers through his short strands. "Speaking of which, I love our daughter dearly, but she's a wee bit fussy. So kiss me whilst you have the chance, Jake. Because otherwise, we'll have to wait, and I know I don't want that."

With a growl, he crushed his lips against hers as he lowered his hot, solid body. The instant his warm skin touched hers, she moaned and took the kiss deeper, needing this male, almost as if she might die if she didn't.

Her dragon growled. *Why wait? Flip him over and ride him. It's easy enough.*

Before she could even think of a reply, Jake broke the kiss to lick her jaw, nibble down her throat, and lightly bite where her neck met her shoulder.

Sylvia arched up, her hand on his back, pressing him closer.

His hand trailed down her body, lightly tweaking her nipple, before stroking between her thighs.

Moaning, she moved her hand to his firm arse cheek, gripped him tightly, and tried to press him closer yet again.

Jake chuckled against her shoulder. "Impatient are you?"

She arched her hips, loving how he sucked in a breath as she made contact with his balls and the base of his cock. "Aye, and for good reason. We can do slow and torturous later." When Sophie was a wee bit older, she thought. "For now, just fuck me. Please. You want it as much as I do." She moved against his dick again. "You liked hard and rough with my dragon. Let's do that now."

The hand not on his arse went to his cock. She squeezed, then fondled his sack. With a groan, Jake moved her hand and positioned his dick. With a hard thrust, he filled her, and Sylvia arched into him, moaning.

Then he held her hips down as he moved, each thrust faster than the last, making the bed shake as Sylvia's beast hummed inside her head.

Needing to drive him crazy, she lightly scored her nails down his back. And just as she remembered, it made him growl and grow more frantic.

Then he took her lips, his tongue exploring her

mouth, tangling, thrusting, making her breathless in a good way.

When his fingers found her clit and pressed harder, she moaned. All it took were a few rough, quick strokes, and she fell apart, light dancing in front of her eyes as pleasure surged through her body at the same time as she gripped his cock.

Still reeling from her high, she barely noticed Jake still and cry out before collapsing on top of her.

They both lay like that, breathless and languid, for who knew how long. Sylvia slowly stroked his back, reveling in his heat and the slight sheen of sweat on his skin, inhaling the musky scent that was purely Jake.

It was the little things like this—laying with a male above her as they both caught their breaths—that she'd missed most over the years. The little intimacies she'd once taken for granted.

No. She wasn't going to get overly attached. Sex with Jake was fantastic and had relaxed them both. That had to be enough.

Her dragon said sleepily, *I want more, though. Don't you? Imagine him here every night, his strong arms around us as we sleep.*

Stop it, dragon. You're not helping. Besides, you're the one telling me to live in the moment.

Living in the moment is brilliant. However, you tend to go all in or keep someone at a distance, with nothing in the middle.

I'm just trying to remind you that it's possible for more, but you have to work for it, unafraid to accept a little closeness without obsessing over it.

You're just on cloud nine from the orgasm and not making any sense. Go to sleep.

Her beast yawned. *Fine. For now.*

Jake rolled off her, and she nearly hauled him back, wanting just a little more time without reality seeping in.

But he propped his head on his arm and looked down at her, searching her face for something she couldn't name. He finally brushed a few stray hairs off her cheek as he said, "Tell me something about yourself I don't know."

She blinked at the sudden question. "Like what?"

The corner of his mouth ticked up. "I don't know. It can be silly or serious. Whatever you want. But as much as I already know I like this." He gently cupped between her thighs and winked. "I want to know more of this." He moved his hand to her breast, where her heart thumped wildly. "And this." His hand then cupped her head.

And there the human went, being charming and a wee bit romantic.

Guarding her heart so she didn't fall completely in love with him too soon was going to take more work than she'd originally thought.

Still, no matter what happened, he was Sophie's

father. He should know her somewhat, if for no other reason than that.

Clearing her throat, she replied, "I've never been outside the UK."

He studied her a beat before asking, "But I sense you wanted to travel at some point?"

She nodded. "My late mate—his name was Arthur—and I had planned to do it after the children were grown."

"But then he passed away."

She bobbed her head. "I suppose I could've gone on my own eventually. But I just never bothered."

"Because of your children?"

"Aye, partially." She paused a beat and decided to be fully honest and not lie through omission, although she couldn't quite meet his gaze as she did it. "However, it was more than that, I think. My late mate was murdered, aye? And, well, it took me a long time to come to terms with that."

He traced her cheek and then gently made her meet his gaze again. "Sorry isn't enough of a word to make up for what you went through."

Even though he didn't ask how Arthur had died, the question hung in the air.

The evening was turning quite serious, and yet a part of her wanted to get this all out of the way. Almost as if telling Jake about it would help lighten her load a little, maybe even take some of the still lingering grief off her shoulders.

And if she did that, she could focus more on Sophie and ensuring her daughter could see her father in the future.

So she took a deep breath, willed herself not to cry, and explained, "Arthur's best friend went missing, you see. And even though Arthur managed my restaurant and wasn't any sort of Protector, he had promised his friend's mate he'd do whatever he could to help find him." She looked over Jake's shoulder to some far point on the wall, remembering how she'd begged him to stay home. Pushing the memory aside, she continued, "And, well, Arthur took his vows seriously. He said he knew of a place from when they were lads, a place few would ever think to check, and went looking. Except he never came back. It was two days later when they found Arthur and his friend, both in their dragon forms and completely drained of blood." Her voice hitched, but she couldn't help but whisper, "Someone had cared more about making a few quid selling their blood than the lives of two dragonmen and everyone who cared for them."

If only dragon-shifter blood didn't have healing properties. They would've left Arthur alone and he'd still be alive.

Jake moved to pull her close, but she put a hand on his chest and kept him back. "It didn't end there."

He took her hand and waited as Sylvia did her best to blink back her tears. She was going to reveal one of her greatest failures—being unable to care for her children as she should have—and it wasn't going to be easy.

Her inner beast murmured soothing nonsense, which did help a little. Finally, taking a deep breath, she carried on. "Arthur's death hit me hard. I've always struggled with depression. But after mating him and then with the liveliness of my children, my bouts were few and far between. But his death...aye, well, it all came crashing back. I couldn't get out of bed, I could barely string two thoughts together, and I just wanted to hide from the world." She swallowed. "Including my children.

"Oh, they tried to bring me food and cheer me up. But I was always crying, or sleeping, or just trying my best to avoid the ever-present darkness that wanted to take me over completely."

It had been the worst time of her life, far worse than even when her parents died.

But as much as she didn't want to reveal how her children had saved her and not herself, Sylvia pushed on, determined to finish the memory for Jake. "I was that way for weeks, just over a month, actually. If not for my eldest, Cat, I don't know how long it would've gone on."

He squeezed her hand and asked softly, "How did Cat help?"

She finally met his eyes again. But instead of

judgment, or disappointment, or any other number of negative emotions, all she saw was curiosity.

The sight gave her the strength to continue. "She said invoices were due for the restaurant and that if I didn't get out of bed to pay them, she and her siblings would carry me out of bed to do so." She smiled at the memory of teenage Cat taking charge. "She was only fifteen but still determined to keep our family together and strong. And whilst you may not know her well yet, Cat has a certain tone and look in her eye that when it happens, you know she's not bluffing. She would've had them all cart me out of the bedroom, out the door, and all the way to the restaurant too."

Not for the first time, Sylvia was glad Cat had found Lachlan and now had someone to look after her as her daughter deserved.

She continued, "The sight of my teenage daughter trying to take charge, trying to keep our family going, was what finally snapped me out of it. I wasn't exactly happy for a long while after that—and Cat helped me raise her siblings for years—but I was able to at least function somewhat. It took everything I had to help my family, and traveling was the farthest thing from my mind. In fact, going to Glasgow last year was the greatest distance I've been from Lochguard in over a decade." She sighed. "And so, in a very long, roundabout way, that is my answer to your question as to why I haven't traveled."

She waited to see how Jake would react to her tale. It was probably something better reserved for days or weeks later, but she and Jake didn't have that sort of time. And they'd sort of skipped the usual course of dates and things, considering they already had a daughter together.

He brought her fingers to his lips and kissed them. "We all have pasts, Sylvia. But they help shape us to become who we are, right? I'm sorry you've endured such hardship, but I do think you're being harsher on yourself than you need to be. It's clear you love your children and they love you fiercely back, and that's what matters right here, right now." He brought their clasped hands to his chest. "But if you were trying to scare me off, it didn't work. I'm still here."

She tried to think of how to reply to that when Sophie's cry rent the air.

Out of habit, she moved to get up, but Jake gently laid a hand on her shoulder. "I'll check on her."

He kissed her gently, quickly removed the condom, put on his boxers, and left.

And alone once again, all Sylvia could do was try not to think of how nice it was to have someone helping her, easing the burden of being both mother and father to even just one of her children.

Because that had been the hardest aspect of raising her five older kids, once she'd managed to contain her grief for Arthur to a somewhat manageable level. Her late mate had been the steady rock, the lively focus, of their little family. Sylvia hadn't been ready to step into that role but had been forced into it, to make do.

Even brushing aside the nice feeling of Jake's support, Sylvia still couldn't believe the human didn't seem disgusted or disappointed in what she'd revealed about the lowest point of her life.

Between his support and seeming acceptance, old Sylvia would think too much of it. Instead, she decided to harden her heart a little and dismiss it as nothing more than him being nice.

Aye, nice. And still high from his recent orgasm.

That had to be it.

JAKE HURRIED down the hall to check on his daughter, wishing he could've had a few more minutes with Sylvia to talk about her revelations.

She thought of herself as a failure and was being much harsher on herself than she should be. True, he didn't know why she hadn't asked for help from friends or family after her mate's death. Or why her daughter had ended up being the one to help her mother when she needed it most instead of her in-laws, whom Sylvia's kids had talked about briefly during the card game.

He hated not knowing everything he should about the dragonwoman. Jake was used to knowing everything, being the one in charge, and fixing things in his life.

And in the present, he knew nearly nothing, was a human on a dragon clan, and didn't know if he had the power to do much of anything.

Except help with his daughter.

So as he entered, he approached the crib and murmured, "Now, now, Sophie dear, why're you crying?"

He gently picked her up and her tearstained faced twisted his heart. Even though he knew from helping his older sisters with their kids when they were younger that babies often cried, it didn't mean he had to like it.

Placing her over his shoulder, he rubbed her back and said in a soothing tone, "You're all right, little one. I'm so sorry I wasn't here when you were born. But Daddy's here now and I want to make it up to you. And your mom, too." He kissed her cheek. "Let's start by getting you changed and happy again."

As he took care of his daughter, she babbled nonsense and made him smile, her tears forgotten.

At this point in his life, he hadn't imagined he'd be a father. But even though he'd only learned of the fact earlier in the day—had it only been a day?—he wanted to do whatever it took to be there for Sophie.

The trick, though, would be finding what could make him, Sylvia, and Sophie happy together.

And he had no damn idea how to do it.

Unlike with his restaurants, he couldn't plan in advance, make detailed goals, and see it through. Children and women were different and far less predictable.

But he needed to get to know the people of Lochguard better, spend time with both Sylvia and Sophie, and maybe even call his cousin for some advice on how to deal with dragons in general.

Because his cousin's packet hadn't included dating advice or how to better know five grown dragon-shifter children of a woman with whom you had a child.

One of whom was about to have a child of her own, which would make Sylvia a grandmother.

His life really had become like a soap opera, hadn't it?

At least discovering the Uno cards tucked into one of the zippers in his suitcase—there from his visit with one of his sisters a few weeks ago—had been lucky. The card game had been a good start to better know the MacAllisters—it had always cheered his family up—but it wasn't enough.

Jake was definitely in new territory, but that wasn't a deterrent. He liked challenges and would face this one head-on.

Once Sophie was changed, he sat with her in the

rocking chair in the corner. Soon she fell asleep cradled in his lap, and Jake didn't have the heart to move her. And so he dozed, the soft weight of his daughter laying on him, and tried to think of how to tackle the next day. Hell, how to approach the next weeks, months, and possibly the entire next phase of his life.

Chapter Seven

The next morning Sylvia found Jake sleeping in the rocking chair with Sophie cradled in his lap and took a second to memorize the scene.

Sylvia had fallen asleep shortly after Jake had gone to check on their daughter. It seemed she had Jake to thank for getting even more sleep after her nap.

And it only made it clearer how much Sylvia had been struggling to take care of Sophie on her own. Maybe if she were in her twenties instead of forties, she'd have had enough energy to do it without a problem. However, while she wasn't an aged decrepit yet, she wasn't exactly as spritely as she once had been.

Sophie must've realized her food source was near because she woke and gave a half-hearted cry. Her father stirred, but Sylvia scooped up Sophie and placed a hand on Jake's shoulder. "Go get some proper rest. I'll take care of her now."

He blinked sleepily up at her. It was barely dawn, and even though the time change had probably screwed up his internal clock, she had a feeling he wasn't usually a morning person anyway. Running restaurants—especially those in big cities like San Francisco—meant working late into the night.

Still, he tried to blink his eyes a few times. His voice heavy with sleep, he said, "I'm fine. I can stay up to help you."

She smiled. "Aye, I know you could. But get some actual sleep, Jake. Yesterday was a long day, after all." He opened his mouth to protest again, but she added, "Besides, I was thinking of an outing today, aye? And I can't have you asleep if we do that."

He stretched his arms above his head, some of his joints popping. "An outing, you say?"

She nodded. "Aye. But I won't say more until you get some sleep first. Think of it as an incentive. Well, if you like surprises. Which, admittedly, I don't know if you do."

And just like that, Sylvia was back to doubting everything again.

Her dragon said, *Stop worrying.*

Jake spoke before she could reply to her beast. "Most of the time, yes, I like surprises." He searched her gaze as he stood, as if he was trying to figure out what she had planned. However, Sylvia merely raised her brows and shook her head to say she wouldn't tell. He finally sighed. "Okay, I can see you're not going to tell me anything, no matter what. But just don't let me sleep the whole day. I want to spend more time with Sophie."

A part of her still couldn't believe Jake had accepted his unexpected child so easily. She really did need to learn more about his family.

However, her daughter moved her mouth in a way that told her she was hungry. So Sylvia settled in the chair and lifted her shirt. Once Sophie began suckling, she replied, "Aye, of course I'll make sure you don't sleep the day away. Now, off to bed with you."

He smiled at her half-hearted order before kissing her cheek, touching Sophie's head, and then stumbling out the door, revealing how tired he still was.

She hummed, and in no time at all, she'd fed Sophie, changed her, and headed downstairs with her youngest in tow. Sylvia had barely started making breakfast when she heard the front door opened and a few beats later, Emma walked into the kitchen.

Emma looked around slowly and wiped her brow dramatically. "Whew, good, it's safe. I don't need to walk in on my mum and her male going at it like rabbits in the kitchen."

She growled, "Emma Lucia."

Her middle daughter grinned at the use of her

middle name. "I'm allowed to poke fun. I already told you I like him." Emma swiped an orange from the bowl of fruit on the counter and began peeling it. "Although you look heaps better today, Mum. I don't care if it's having help or a magical healing cock that did it, but I'm glad."

Sylvia sighed and decided ignoring Emma's prods to be the best course of action. "You all helped as much you could. But Sophie melts in Jake's hands, so aye, it's been nice having him here."

"And not for his odds-defying human cock? I hope you used what I left in your room. Otherwise, it may take just the one night for me to get another sibling."

Her dragon laughed, but Sylvia ignored her inner beast. She merely stared at her cheeky daughter a moment before deciding to ask something neutral. "Why are you here so early, Emma? You never get up so close to dawn at this time of year."

Emma shrugged. "I have something to do today that requires an early start. And no, I'm not telling you what it is. It won't kill me, though. And Logan, as well as the MacKay brothers from Seahaven, are going with me too."

At the mention of Logan, Sylvia resisted a frown. She'd long ago noticed that Logan Lamont loved—or at least thought he was in love with—Emma. Her daughter, on the other hand, seemed oblivious. She thought of him only as a friend, like a brother.

Maybe Sylvia needed to talk to Logan and see why the poor lad tortured himself. He'd had a hard enough time with his brother's years-long disappearance. Aye, his brother had come back with his mate in tow, and the two brothers were close again. But still. The lad deserved someone who appreciated him.

Her dragon snorted. *And you tell Emma not to meddle.*

I rarely meddle. But Logan needs to move on. Emma has no interest in him, and he deserves better than to hold on to hope. After all, he knows they're not true mates.

And that doesn't always matter. You mated Arthur at seventeen, without knowing if he was our true mate. Aye, it worked out that way in the end, learning it was true when we hit twenty, but even if it hadn't, it wouldn't have mattered.

Male dragons could recognize their true mates—their supposed best chances at happiness—once both parties were at least twenty. It was part of the reason her own father had tried to convince her to wait to mate Arthur.

But in the end, she'd prevailed. And her beast was right—she wouldn't have cared if Arthur hadn't been her true mate or not. She replied, *But Emma and Logan aren't me and Arthur. The lad wants a family. I can tell by the looks he gives his brother, mate, and child when he thinks no one is looking. Emma is far from that point. She thinks having a bairn means pawning it off on a relative to watch it.*

Emma's voice interrupted her conversation with

her beast. "If you're planning a rescue party with your dragon, just stop. I won't be going further south than Inverness, and I know these lands."

Sylvia forced herself to focus on the present. "Faye and Grant cleared your outing?"

She nodded. "Aye. One of the MacKay brothers is a Protector. Add in that Logan is a nurse, and we have the bases covered—both security and medical care." Emma finished her orange and added, "Besides, I'm more interested in what you're going to do today, Mum. Are you going to stay home and ravish your human whenever Sophie's asleep?"

Sylvia rolled her eyes. "No. I'm going to show him my restaurant and maybe go to the old stone broch nearby, if the weather is good enough."

"The broch? The one where young couples go for a stolen kiss, to make a wish? Or maybe to go and see Jamie's legendary spirit?"

Her youngest son claimed there was truth to the old legend of Loch Naver and the spirit who guarded it. For once she was glad her children weren't all under one roof since Jamie's siblings teased him to no end about it. "If the spirit shows, then that'd be brilliant. But I just thought to share a bit of Lochguard with Jake. Being spring, the weather isn't great, and I can't exactly take him up to the coast or to the Isle of Skye without probably facing lots of wind and rain."

Emma grunted. "Aye, I suppose." She went to the

refrigerator and took out the ingredients for sandwiches. "I'm going to make some lunch to take with us. Do you need some?"

"No, thank you. Although if you could keep an eye on your sister whilst I finish cooking breakfast, that would be great."

And so, as they went about normal routines, it was hard to imagine much had changed from a few days before.

But it had. And not just because Sylvia kept smiling as she remembered Jake's kisses or him sleeping with Sophie in his arms.

Her mood was better than it had been in ages. And Sylvia was determined to make the best of it.

Chapter Eight

After leaving Sophie safely with Ian, Jake and Sylvia had gone to the restaurant. Jake deemed it a decent size—maybe sixty or seventy people could sit at the tables inside and several more at the counter. And the place had a fair amount of charm with artwork of dragons and landscapes on the walls, as well as cheery colors of yellow or light blue for tablecloths, and vases of flowers on every table.

While it was a long way from the more refined elegance of his establishments back in San Fran, it suited what he'd seen of Lochguard so far. Homey and comfortable were more important than rich, refined decorations.

To be honest, it reminded him of his early days, when he'd still been working his way up the chain at a small, family-owned restaurant as he finished culinary school.

Sylvia had just finished giving Jake his tour and had gestured for him to take a seat near the window for some tea and lunch when an older woman—the one who had come up to him the day before to ask if he'd come to see Sophie—walked up to him and asked, "So are you staying around now? Or will you abandon poor Sylvia to raise the child alone?"

He was about to ask who the rude woman was when Sylvia said, "Don't, Meg. Just leave it, aye?"

Meg huffed. "No, I won't. Poor lassie, raising a child all by herself, and at your age too. And then he comes waltzing in and gives no promises. Not how it was done in my day, not at all."

A fair younger man—no, dragonman, judging by his tattoo—and a woman with black, curly hair and brown skin raced up and stopped next to Meg. It was the dragonman who said, "Leave them alone, Mum."

Meg bristled. "I can't do that, Alistair, so don't ask me to. Sylvia doesn't have a mother to watch out for her, so someone has to be there for her."

Jake cleared his throat, garnering Meg's attention. "And who, might I ask, are you?"

The dragonwoman raised her brows. "I'm Meg Boyd, of course. One of the ones looking after young Sylvia."

Jake didn't care for liars, and he could already tell Meg was one of them. He stood, leaned close to

Meg, and murmured so the other ears at nearby tables wouldn't be able to hear his words. "Looking after her, are you? Then where were you yesterday? Or the day before? I think you've never come by to help once, am I right?" The older woman opened her mouth and then shut it. He leaned back and spoke in a normal tone. "Now, if you don't mind, we're about to have lunch. So if you'd excuse us."

Meg looked to say something, but the dragonman at her side turned her away. "Come, Mum." He then nodded at Jake. "I'm Alistair Boyd. Sorry about my mother. She won't bother your lunch."

As he guided Meg away, the dark-haired woman approached him and smiled. "Good, someone needs to deal with Meg on occasion. Too many people are bloody afraid of her." She put her hand out. "I'm Kiyana Boyd, Alistair's mate, and one of the humans living here."

He shook her hand. "I'm Jake Swift."

She nodded and reached for something in her bag. Then she scribbled and handed him a piece of paper. "If you need any help, or have questions, call me. I've worked for the Department of Dragon Affairs for years and like helping other humans adjust." She lowered her voice. "And don't worry, Alistair and I don't live with his mother, so you won't have to chance bumping into her. We also have a young daughter, so maybe when Sophie's a bit older, they can play together."

He took the paper and smiled at her. Even if he didn't know her, his gut said she was honest and would be true to her word. "Thank you." He raised it. "I'll call if I need it."

Kiyana smiled at him and then Sylvia before racing after her mate and mother-in-law.

He noticed others in the room glancing at them, but Jake decided to ignore their stares and focused on Sylvia as he sat back down. "I didn't want to start gossip, but I couldn't let her act high and mighty when I know for a fact she hasn't been helping you."

The dragonwoman's cheeks turned pink. "Meg means well."

"Perhaps. But her words have me thinking." He kept his voice low again, wishing they were somewhere more private. "From what your kids told me, you have a lot of in-laws. I get the impression they didn't help you after your mate's death. Why?"

She fiddled with the silverware a few beats before she murmured, "Not here. Let's go to my office."

He followed her out of the main dining area, down a hall, and into a medium-sized room with a desk, a few bookcases along the wall, and small sofa against another wall. Once the door closed, she leaned against her desk. Jake raised his brows in question, and she finally spoke. "Let me start by saying we've all reconciled and it's no longer an issue."

He raised his brows. "That's not an answer, Sylvia."

She sighed. "I know. But I wanted to set the scene, so you won't get too angry, aye?"

Jake didn't like the sound of that, but he did his best to keep his expression neutral. "Okay. Then tell me what happened."

She fiddled with a pen on her desk as she said, "Everyone took Arthur's death hard. And as I mentioned, I had trouble with it. I wasn't allowing visitors for the first month, and it sort of angered my in-laws. And when one of Arthur's brothers, Arlo, forced his way in and saw me hiding away in bed, he threatened to take my children away and raise them himself."

Sylvia paused a beat, took a deep breath, and then continued, "Cat and Connor yelled at him and told him to leave. I didn't hear what happened next until later, but apparently, Arlo had said that if he left without my children, they'd all be on their own and the MacAllisters wouldn't help any of us. Cat and Connor had told him fine and shoved him out of the house."

She met his gaze again. "That happened the week before Cat finally got me out of my bedroom. It was weeks before I learned of what had happened, which made the tension worse."

"Because the MacAllisters thought you agreed to sever ties."

She nodded. "Once I was back into a mostly normal routine, I sought them out, and slowly we mended fences. But it took years for any sort of ease to come back."

He took a step toward her and tentatively took her hand. When she didn't pull away, he squeezed gently. "And your own family?"

She shook her head. "My mother died shortly after I was born, and it was just my dad and me. He died a few years before Arthur did, so I didn't have anyone else here to lean on. My mother was from Spain, and I have relatives there, but I've never met them. And I wasn't about to take my children from everything they knew and show up on their doorsteps, hoping they'd help. So I did the best I could here instead. It's part of the reason I relied on Cat so heavily, even once I was back on my feet—I had to run the restaurant on my own and couldn't be a full-time mother."

As far as Jake knew, clan leaders were supposed to help everyone under their protection. He asked about it and Sylvia gave a sad smile. "The leader before Finn was quite a bit different. He didn't like to get in between families unless bloodshed was imminent. So it was pointless to bother him since he'd merely dismiss it as my problem to handle."

The more he learned about Sylvia's circumstances after her mate's murder, the more it angered him. She thought herself a failure, and yet the enormity of what she'd managed to live through was the opposite of it. Almost everyone had abandoned her, and she'd done the best she could to take care of herself and her five children.

And she'd been left to face hardship again by taking care of Sophie alone as well. Sure, her children were there, but the more he learned about Sylvia, the more he realized she wanted to be the one to take care of everyone but herself.

He gently took her chin in his fingers and ensured she maintained eye contact as he said, "More than ever, I'm sorry that I wasn't here for your pregnancy and Sophie's early days. But I promise I'll be around to help you from now on. This time, you won't have to try to take on the world alone."

She smiled sadly. "As much as I'd like that, you have a life back in America, Jake—businesses, family, and friends. I can't ask you to leave it all behind because of some unreliable condoms from a one-night stand." He opened his mouth to protest, but she pushed on before he could. "My mother tried to do that, leaving her family behind in Spain, thinking she'd be fine on a new clan in a foreign land. And as she lay dying soon after I was born, everyone said she wished she'd seen her family and friends in Spain more often." She shook her head. "I don't want that for you. So I hope you'll visit when you can, and that will mean the world to Sophie. But that's all it can be."

He resisted growling at her determination to push him away. Jake wasn't one to make rash decisions. Well, usually. The night with Sylvia had been one of his rare spontaneous exceptions.

However, his restaurants were established and he could hire managers. Some of his family would probably even be willing to move to Scotland if it were possible, to leave behind memories of his late nephew.

Not to mention that with technology, it would be easy enough to contact the friends he cared about.

Because when it came down to it, Jake only had one daughter. Hell, she might be his only child, ever.

And he was damned if he'd visit her once or twice a year, hoping Sophie remembered him each time he showed up.

Somehow, some way, he was going to find a way to be a part of his daughter's life.

However, he sensed that if he said that now, Sylvia would dismiss it as being hasty.

And while it was true, they'd barely spent much time together, Jake trusted his gut. And he wanted to be in his daughter's life more than anything. If he could win her mother, it would be even better.

He knew a teasing, playful woman was inside there somewhere, as he'd seen her a year ago in Glasgow. He had a feeling that side of Sylvia would come out again if given the chance.

He'd just have to woo her slowly. Prove he meant

to be there for her and Sophie to lean on, until she didn't doubt him.

Until she didn't think he'd leave when it became inconvenient. Or abandon her like many of those she'd loved over the years had done at one point or another.

Mind made up, he finally replied, "For now, we have these two weeks." He leaned closer, until his lips were a few inches from hers. "Tell me you'll give me those, at least, Sylvia. To better know both you and Sophie." He lightly caressed her cheek, her soft, warm skin making his heart beat faster. He murmured, "Because I know last night wasn't enough for me."

Her pupils flashed to slits and back before she whispered, "Sophie, of course, you should know. I'm not as sure about us."

"And what does your dragon say?"

She hesitated as her pupils flashed some more. Eventually, she sighed and said, "She sides with you. Of course she does."

His lips twitched. "You sound irritated about it."

She harrumphed. "Anything with a cock would make her happy."

He chuckled. "And you're reminding me yet again of how much I love your inner beast."

She tried not to smile and failed. "She mostly likes you, I should say. She's rather upset about you not seeing her in her dragon form yet."

"We could do that now, while Ian still has Sophie." She glanced away and he pushed, "It'll help me get used to seeing dragons, for one thing. And it'll help with my dragon-shifter education. My daughter will be able to shift one day, so I'd better start learning."

He held his breath as he waited for Sylvia to reply. His first instinct was to keep pushing until she said yes.

But it seemed like everyone tried to push her around or even tried to roll over her. First her in-laws, and then Meg Boyd. Sometimes even her five grown-up children did it too.

He'd much rather gently nudge Sylvia and let her shine on her own. After all, he suspected no one else thought that was what she needed.

He could be wrong, but Jake would amend his plans as he went.

She finally let out a long breath and nodded. "Aye, I should show you my dragon form. Because if I wait too long, one of my children will cart you off to shift for you, and I suspect they'll forget all of their manners when they do and merely try to scare you."

He chuckled. "They could try. But I think Emma likes me, at least. And I'm working on Jamie."

She searched his gaze. "Why are you trying so hard with them?"

He shrugged one shoulder. "They're Sophie's family, which makes them my family too, in a way. I haven't had a chance to tell you much about my sisters, nieces, and nephews, but they're important to me. It's why I didn't come to Lochguard sooner."

"Then let's make that our deal—you tell me what kept you and then I'll show you my dragon."

"Only if we can eat at the same time. I won't have you fainting again."

She bit her lip. "That was a one-off."

"Regardless, ensuring you eat and sleep enough is the least I can do for the gift of giving me a daughter, Sylvia."

She opened her mouth and then closed it. After a few seconds, she finally murmured, "I put in an order with Connor earlier so it should be ready. Wait here. I'll be right back."

Sylvia left, and he walked around the room, wanting to learn a little more about his dragonwoman's everyday life. Both because he wanted to know, but it also helped distract him. Talking about Nick's death wasn't easy, even after all these months. But if Sylvia could share her grief, depression, and family troubles after her mate's murder, he could do this too.

SYLVIA TRIED to ignore the warmth in her chest as she remembered Jake's words and touch.

Trying to resist him and convince him not to give

up everything for her was going to be difficult. And yet, she didn't want him to resent her for the rest of his life.

Her mother had loved her father, from what everyone said. But she'd still grown sadder by the day the longer she lived away from her family.

Some said her sadness, even more than her complications from childbirth, had ultimately caused her mother's death.

And Sylvia wouldn't cause that sort of regret or sadness for Jake, especially since neither of them was in love to begin with.

Oh, aye, Sylvia could see herself falling for him in time—who wouldn't want the charming, supportive, successful human—but she was doing her best to guard her heart. Sophie depended on her, as did her other children, full-grown or not. They were what mattered, in the end.

As she picked up their lunch orders from the kitchen and headed back toward her office, her dragon couldn't keep quiet any longer. *I still don't understand why you keep trying to push Jake away. If he wants to stay here, it's his choice. You shouldn't worry about the worst outcome possible.*

I have to worry. The only way Jake could stay on Lochguard is if he were to mate me. And I don't want it forced.

Her beast sniffed. *He's a grown male. Let him make his own choices.*

*You only say that because you want him to share our bed
every night.*

*Day, too. But that's not the only reason. It's nice to have a
partner again, someone to help share the burden.*

Sophie's not *a burden.*

*Maybe not a burden, but a lot of work. And he seems to
love taking care of her.*

That part Sylvia wouldn't argue with. Even if it
were early days and he might grow more disheveled
and irritated as time wore on due to lack of sleep or
peace, she was glad Sophie had this time with her
father.

Strange as it was, her daughter seemed to
instinctively know Jake was her dad and loved being
with him. He seemed to radiate a calming sort of
confidence, one that Sylvia couldn't seem to manage.

She'd forgotten what it was like to raise a child
with a supportive mate at her side.

Her dragon grunted. *If it's a supportive mate you
want, give him a chance.*

Sylvia was nearly back to her office, so she said
quickly to her beast, *I promised him these two weeks. Just
accept that for now, aye?*

Fine.

As her dragon curled up to nap, Sylvia entered
her office, laid the plates down on either side of the
desk, and shut the door.

Jake turned from his place by the window and
smiled. The crinkles at the corner of his eyes made

her heart skip a beat. "Did you create the small, walled garden just outside this window, or did it come that way with the building?"

She glanced at the wee slice of paradise, the one she loved to sit in during a break or a slow time, to simply enjoy the scents of the flowers and any sunshine that happened to make an appearance. "Arthur originally built it for me, and we filled it out together. Although in recent years, Ian and Connor have maintained it."

He gestured toward the seat in front of the desk. "Let's eat and I'll tell you why I didn't come looking for you sooner."

She nearly blinked at the change of topic. At least she wouldn't have to badger him to get an answer.

Jake waited until she sat and took the first bite of her sandwich before he sat across from her. "I'll start by saying I have two much older sisters—I was a surprise for my parents, born eight years after their last child—and it was my eldest sister, Lila, who took me in at fifteen when our parents were killed in a car crash."

She itched to ask for details but somehow knew this wasn't yet the point of his story. So Sylvia nodded. He eyed her sandwich again. Looking toward the ceiling—really, he'd just revealed his parents had died when he was still a child, and he wanted her to eat—she picked it up and ate another bite.

After he smiled at her a second, he continued, "Growing up, it had always been hard to really get to know my sisters since they are eleven and eight years older than me. But living with Lila after my parents' deaths, well, we grew close. I was there when her first child learned to walk and saw her next two children the day they each respectively came home from the hospital. In the end, I lived there four years before I moved out.

"And when Lila's husband died of cancer a few years ago, me and Ada—our other sister—grew even closer. We all helped Lila when we could and did our best to make her children laugh or smile. And everything was going great again. We'd even planned a big camping trip for this upcoming summer, with everyone all together for once, which was a big deal since Lila's son Nick was in the Marines and hadn't been home much since he joined at eighteen." He paused, tapped his hand against the desk a few times, and said, "And then word came of Nick's missing in action. At first, everyone held out hope. But as time went on, it faded. The military eventually sent their condolences, saying they'd confirmed his death." He met her gaze head-on. "It destroyed my eldest sister, her two daughters, Nick's wife, and the family as a whole."

Her heart ached at the thought of losing one of her sons so young. She couldn't begin to imagine what Lila had gone through. "When did that happen?"

He sighed. "About eight months ago, two weeks before I had decided to come to Scotland and talk with you. But I couldn't leave then. I had to stay and keep everyone together. Even though I'm the youngest, I was always the sort of peacekeeper between everyone as adults. And while my sister will never be fine with the loss of her son, she's doing a little better these days. The same with Nick's sisters and Nick's wife. So I was finally able to come seek you out." He leaned forward. "Do know that I wish I could've come here sooner, back when I had originally planned to."

Sylvia shook her head. "Don't worry about that. Of course you needed to help your family." She bit her lip and then blurted, "I'm surprised you left them to chase the female who slipped away during the night without a word."

He never broke his gaze as he replied, "Certain people leave an impression, and you were one of them. I don't like what-ifs. I spent too much of my time as a late teen wondering about how things could've been different if my parents had lived." He reached out and took one of her hands. "It's why I'm here, and I'm glad I came. Not only for the beautiful, caring, kind dragonwoman, either. I didn't realize how much I wanted a child until I held Sophie for the first time."

Her cheeks heated at his words. Not only for the compliments, but for the fact he was as grateful for Sophie as she was.

Aye, well, nearly so. She decided to blurt the truth she hadn't yet told him. "I'm grateful for Sophie, too, in more ways than one. Remember how I said I was ill?" He nodded. "The doctors couldn't figure out exactly what was wrong with me. My blood tests indicated some of my organs were failing, among other things. They were at wit's end trying to figure out what caused it and how to save me. But in the end, Sophie was the one who did it. The doctors think her human hormones helped me in some way and reversed the decline. I haven't had a poor result since I became pregnant. And even if they haven't pinpointed the illness exactly, it's made Dr. MacFarland realize the further potential of human hormones in helping dragon-shifters." She paused a second to clear the emotion from her throat before whispering, "So without Sophie, I might not be alive right now. I'm more grateful than I could ever believe for the wee surprise you left me."

He squeezed her hand. "And I'm grateful that you're still here too."

As they stared at one another, something shifted inside Sylvia. Oh, she wanted this male. It would be so easy to care for him, to grow addicted to his smiles and the way he seemed to put her at ease without even trying.

Not to mention he made her skin heat and desire flood her body with a mere touch.

But rather than think of a future that probably wouldn't happen, she withdrew her hand and changed the subject back to Jake's family. "So will you still have a family camping trip this year?"

He raised his brows at her sudden question but then settled back in his chair. "I don't think so. To be honest, in the aftermath of Nick's death, I think we all forgot about it. Although…"

His voice trailed off, and she nudged, "What?"

"Well, do you like camping?"

She blinked. "Camping? It's not something dragon-shifters usually do, unless they're on the run. After all, we can easily fly somewhere for the day and come back." She searched his face a beat. "Why?"

He smiled. "I was thinking maybe I could fly my sisters, brother-in-law, nephew and nieces, and Nick's wife here for a trip."

She frowned. "That would cost a bloody fortune."

Jake shrugged. "I can afford it."

For a second, she wondered if her attractive, charming human was also rich. Not that it mattered to her—she'd been content working in a restaurant for most of her life—but it would still be a bit of a shock. "I don't know. Where would they stay? I doubt the DDA would allow them all to holiday with a dragon clan."

He swallowed his latest bit of sandwich. "Well,

I'm sure there has to be somewhere we can all stay together, maybe rent some cottages or something instead of camping. I'd like them to meet you and Sophie. No matter what happens, you'll still be family. And you can invite your children too."

For a second, she wondered how it'd be to have a family gathering without all of the MacAllister in-laws trying to outdo each other for the spotlight. One where she might actually get to play hostess without her in-laws stepping on her toes, or how it would feel to not wonder if someone was thinking about Arthur anytime they saw her.

Her dragon said softly, *It'll be nice for his family, too, to be somewhere new, some place that doesn't constantly remind them of the lad they lost.*

But Cat's bairn is due anytime now, aye?

Ask him about the details before making a decision.

Jake looked at her and waited. She finally said, "It'd have to be after my daughter has her bairn. She's due in the next couple of weeks."

"It wouldn't be until May or June anyway, and that's eight, ten, or even twelve weeks away, depending on the date. Cat and her mate might not be able to do more than a day trip with a new baby, or maybe it would be old enough to stay in a cottage with them. We'll figure something out, I promise. What do you think?"

Despite the nervousness bouncing around her stomach at the thought of meeting all of Jake's family, Sylvia bobbed her head. "If it's the end of June, then Cat and Lachlan could probably come. Dragon-shifters tend to recover quickly after birth, at least after the first week or so post-delivery."

She refused to think her daughter would be one of the females who got an infection and died, like her mother had.

No, Cat was strong. And stubborn. Her daughter would—had to—live.

Jake smiled. "Sounds perfect, as I'm sure the weather will be better then anyway. From what I've heard, August or early September might be the warmest, but I can't wait that long." He rubbed his hands together, and the joy in his eyes made Sylvia smile wider.

For a male in his forties, he had the excitement of a child at times. And she had a feeling if she were around it often enough, it'd be infectious.

Jake finally added, "Then I just need to find a place where humans and dragons can stay together. Maybe your clan leader would know of one?"

"Finn probably would." She paused and asked, "Just how many people would be coming?"

"My sisters and their families would be eight, and with Nick's wife—she has no other family and we've unofficially adopted her—would make nine. Although my cousin Ashley, her mate, and their son might want to come. That might be trickier, though. How do dragon-shifters do on airplanes?"

Good question. "I've never experienced it myself, but usually any dragon-shifter of shifting age has to be drugged unconscious or have their dragon silenced for the flight."

He tapped his hand on the desk, a sign she was coming to understand meant he was thinking. "Once we're done here, I'll talk to Finn before I head back toward your cottage." He smiled. "If I can make it work, it might be just what my family needs." He leaned over and lowered his voice conspiratorially. "Maybe one of your sons or daughter will hit it off with one of my nieces or nephew. They're all in their twenties now, so who knows."

She snorted. "I doubt it as none of my older children are looking. But I wouldn't mention it or even tease about it, or Ian will flat-out refuse to come. He doesn't always act it when it's just with family, but he's the shyest of all my children, and facing so many new people will make him want to hide behind his work."

He chuckled. "I won't even tease about it. It's more important for everyone to relax, get to know each other, and have fun. So let's hurry and finish eating so I can talk to Finn. Once I get an idea in my head, I itch to see it come true."

She ate a few chips from her plate before asking, "You do that for your restaurants, aye? Go full tilt to see if a new idea will work."

"Of course."

And as he went into detail about the changes he'd made in decorations or menus, Sylvia enjoyed listening to his warm, deep, passionate voice.

So many things seemed to make Jake animated and full of smiles or grins. She rather liked that about him.

Almost as if seeing his joy stoked a little of her own.

Not that she wanted to think of that. The last male to have that ability, albeit more through teasing than anything else, had been her late mate. But she and Jake weren't more than co-parents who sometimes slept together.

Her dragon snorted but remained quiet.

When they both finished eating and Jake left to talk to Finn, Sylvia nearly jumped to follow him. They'd been together almost constantly for the last two days, and it was strange to not have him near.

That realization rang further warning bells inside her head.

Her dragon sighed. *Stop worrying. Just enjoy him and have fun.*

While she gathered their empty plates and tried to tell herself she could do that, Connor came in and thankfully distracted her with restaurant business for the next hour or so.

Chapter Nine

Once Jake had an idea in his head, he did everything he could to see if it would work. And if so, see it through.

Finn had liked his idea of inviting his family to come to meet Sophie. Although instead of going somewhere near Lochguard, he'd suggested staying in a collection of cottages not far from Clan Stonefire down in the Lake District in England. The DDA didn't mind if dragon-shifters stayed there due to some decades-old agreement made between Stonefire and the British government, and humans could stay freely as well, since it was mostly humans who rented the cottages.

The dragonman had quickly called the Stonefire clan leader, booked dates Jake thought would work, and then directed him to a room with a phone he could use.

Inside of three hours, he'd booked and coordinated everything. Thanks to a family vacation to Costa Rica two years ago, everyone already had passports. And his sisters had thought it a good idea to get away—they'd kept the dates for the original camping trip blocked out for some sort of family time —although they didn't like him footing the bill.

He'd assured them they could help with meals and the like once in England, or help take care of Sophie. The revelation of his daughter had been a little awkward, but both Lila and Ada had been happy in the end. They wanted a niece to spoil. Lila, in particular, had sounded more animated than he'd heard her since Nick's death.

Although they didn't like his evasive answers about what he planned to do with Sophie's mother. However, Jake was still working on that himself and he didn't need his sisters trying to meddle.

The only people who hadn't confirmed yet were Ashley, her mate, and their son. Something about Wes—Ashley's mate—needing time to think about it. Since Wes was a dragon clan leader, Jake understood the man couldn't just up and leave on a whim; it would take a tremendous amount of planning.

But he hoped his favorite cousin and her family would make it eventually, especially since he'd hinted at how it'd give Ashley and Wes the chance to better know a few clan leaders in the UK.

With everything planned out, he headed back

toward Sylvia's cottage. He hadn't meant to be away so long, but she'd stopped by Finn's place hours ago and had said she could manage a few hours on her own.

Still, he missed her and Sophie and the coziness of their little bubble.

And fuck, if it was this way after only a couple of days, he couldn't imagine what it'd be like at the end of two weeks.

Because he would have to leave and go back to the US to sort out a few things for his restaurants before coming back to Scotland again. And that could take him weeks, or even months, to arrange.

Jake didn't like that one bit.

However, as he reached Sylvia's place, he pushed that thought aside. He'd take what time he could for now and figure out the rest later.

He entered the house to a low hum of conversation. Entering the living room, he spotted Ian, Jamie, and a few older dragon-shifter men he didn't know.

Sylvia noticed him. The tightness of her jaw relaxed as she smiled. "You're back."

He glanced at the unknown people and then went to her side. "Yes, I have everything planned out now. Is Sophie asleep?"

She nodded, but before Sylvia could reply, the elderly dragonman with gray hair and blue eyes the same shade as many of Sylvia's kids grunted and asked, "How do we know it's safe to keep you around my grandkids? For all we know, you could be some undercover spy for the dragon hunters or whatever they're called in America. Has Finn run a background check? I'd like to see it."

He eyed the elderly dragonman a beat. Despite being in his sixth or seventh decade, he was tall and maybe even imposing to the average human. But Jake didn't bat an eye. "And you are?"

The dragonman stood a fraction taller and jabbed his own chest. "I'm Archie MacAllister, father to Sylvia's true mate."

The way the male emphasized "true mate" was a dig at Jake, to be sure.

Sylvia spoke up. "Archie was just about to leave, aye?"

The older man bristled. "Don't try to push me out the door, lassie. Someone has to look out for you."

The fingers of one of Jake's hands curled into a fist. This man was part of the family that had all but abandoned Sylvia when she needed their help the most. And he hadn't seen hide nor hair of the man since Jake had arrived, either. He doubted he helped out with Sophie at all.

Jake's first instinct was to kick the old man out the door, along with the two males who stood next to him.

But as one of the younger men—relatively, given

how they looked older than Jake—placed his hand on Archie's shoulder, he said, "Sorry for my dad. Meg's been in a huff all day and he wants to play the hero."

He glanced at Sylvia and she explained, "Meg Boyd is involved with my father-in-law."

Jake focused on the two males standing to either side of Archie. Given the shapes of their eyes and noses, he bet the third unnamed dragonman was also related. Jake said, "I'm Jake Swift, as you probably know. Who're you guys?"

The dragonman gestured to himself and the other as he said, "Seamus and Arlo MacAllister. Arthur was our younger brother."

More MacAllisters. He eyed Arlo for a few beats, remembering the name from Sylvia's story about him wanting to take away her children without even talking to her about it.

He nodded. "Okay, well, with introductions out of the way, I'm still not sure why you all are here with Sylvia. I dealt with Meg, not her. If there's a problem, you should've come to find me instead."

Archie narrowed his eyes at Jake. "I was hoping she would toss your arse out."

Arlo added, "Or at least convince you to give Meg an apology."

Jake raised an eyebrow. "Why?"

Everyone blinked at his question. Seamus looked at Sylvia. "You know what Meg could do, if she carries a grudge, Sylvia."

Jake glanced at her and could see indecision in her eyes.

And in that moment, he noticed quite a lot. It seemed everyone kept trying to enforce their wills on Sylvia in the guise of trying to protect her. No wonder she didn't have a chance to relax and laugh, to be the person he'd met in Glasgow the year before. No doubt then she'd had the chance to merely be herself for a change, without living up to people's expectations or demands.

Instead of treasuring her kindness and desire to please, they all took advantage of it.

And Jake wasn't having it. He wouldn't smother Sylvia, but he'd sure as hell do his best to let her breathe and do what she wanted for a change.

He looked at each of the dragonmen in turn as he said, "I won't apologize for speaking the truth. I think it's time for you three to leave. Sylvia and I have plans, and I was already running late."

If Sylvia was confused by his obvious lie—or, rather, fudging the truth as they had planned to hang out with each other again—she didn't show it.

Arlo and Archie glared daggers at him, but Jake didn't flinch. He hadn't become the owner of some of the most sought-after restaurants in the Bay Area by being weak and giving in with a little bit of pressure or intimidation.

Seamus looked apologetic, but Jake was undecided about the dragonman still. If he really felt that way, he should stand up to his relatives instead of helping to gang up on Sylvia.

Sylvia finally spoke up. "He's right. I think it's time for you all to leave."

All three dragonmen blinked, clearly not expecting her to agree with him.

Jake itched to put an arm around her waist and pull her to his side, but resisted. She didn't need another person trying to make a show of using her as some sort of tool to boost their ego.

Seamus nodded. "Aye, we'll go. Come on, Dad, Arlo."

Archie grunted. "Meg deserves an apology."

Seamus gently nudged his father. "Then talk with Finn about it. For now, it's time to go."

With another glare, Archie finally turned to leave, along with the other two dragonmen.

Once they were alone, Jake turned to face Sylvia. "I know it was a little rude, but I couldn't stand by and let them guilt-trip you into anything."

She smiled at him, pulled his head down, and kissed him gently before she whispered, "Thank you. I wish I had the same courage."

He pressed Sylvia up against him with one hand and cupped her cheek with the other. "Hang out with me long enough and you'll be able to do it in your sleep."

She grinned. "And then I can claim it's some sort of American corruption, aye?"

"Call it whatever you want, as long as you're happy." He kissed the corner of her mouth. "Blame me for all of it." He kissed the other side of her mouth. "But just know I can give you lessons whenever you want."

She laughed and the light sound did something to his heart, making it thump harder.

Damn, he loved it when she laughed. He needed to ensure she did it more often.

For now, he satisfied himself by taking her lips, licking the seam, and groaning as his tongue explored her sweet taste, loving how her tongue shyly met his.

But only for a moment, then they each clung to each other, and the kiss turned fierce, needy, hot—as if neither one could get close enough to the other.

Desire and attraction would never be a problem between them.

But he refused to dwell on any of the obstacles in their way for more than that. Instead, he slowly guided Sylvia to the sofa, lifted her, and sat her on the back of it.

He ran his hand down her body, but before he could even reach her breast, a wail started from upstairs.

Breaking the kiss, he leaned his forehead against hers. Sylvia smiled and said, "And I'm going to have to teach you how to be quicker with a bairn in the house."

He leaned back, tucked a section of hair behind

her ear, and murmured, "Then as soon as Sophie's asleep again, I think you need to give me my first lesson."

She ran her fingers along his jaw, and Jake nearly groaned at her soft touch. "Aye, well, let's see what she needs. Maybe your magical touch can help settle her sooner rather than later."

Stepping back, he took her hand and tugged her off the couch. He winked. "I'll see what I can do."

And as they tended to Sophie, falling into the rhythm they'd already adopted about who did what, Jake couldn't be mad about his daughter's interruption. There was something right about the three of them making a little family. He only hoped he could find a way to keep them together.

Chapter Ten

The next day, Sylvia looked at Emma's open arms and finally handed over wee Sophie. "You sure you'll be okay watching her? I won't be away for long. Less than an hour, I think."

Emma cuddled her sister close. "Aye, I'll be fine, Mum. Don't worry."

Sylvia bit her bottom lip to voice further doubts.

Her dragon sighed. *She's helped us before. She'll be fine.*

But it's Emma, and she's never watched Sophie for more than five minutes on her own before. If it's not work-related, she gets distracted. You know it.

At least give her this chance.

Jake had suggested it, saying how a short time watching Sophie might be good for Emma. Otherwise, they'd have to wait even longer for someone else to be available to watch their daughter so Sylvia could finally show Jake her dragon.

If only he were here to reassure her. But Jake had a few matters to discuss with Finn, apparently, and said he'd meet her at the landing area.

Finally Sylvia stepped back. "Aye, but remember to call if you need anything. Jake will have his phone at all times."

Emma bobbed her head. "Of course, Mum. But Sophie's going to be the best sister ever today, aren't you, lassie?"

Sophie merely drooled onto Emma's arm.

Sylvia smiled. "At least that sets the scene for what's to come." Emma frowned and Sylvia added, "Aye, well, I'll go. I won't be long."

And turning around, Sylvia made her feet move.

Her beast sighed. *Stop worrying. Besides, this is an exciting day for me. So don't try to ruin my mood.*

Her dragon was right—this would be the first time Jake ever saw their dragon form. *I know, I know. It's just strange having so much help these days.*

People, such as the MacKenzies, have often offered help the past three months. You just always refused to accept it for some reason.

Sylvia hated being a burden on anyone. It was one of her greatest faults, made worse by her wanting to prove she could be a good mother to Sophie. *I'm trying my best. And Jake makes it easy to accept help. He has a way of making it seem as if he should've always been around.*

Of course he does. He's sexy, caring, and charming. I still say you should mate him and keep the human around.

Let's not ruin the day by arguing again. I'm doing my best to take it day by day, so I'll leave it there.

Her beast huffed, but fell silent.

It wasn't far to the landing area, and she saw Jake waiting at the edge, near the surrounding rock wall. As soon as he spotted her, he smiled, and her heart skipped a beat.

He really was too handsome for his own good. Not to mention he stood up for her whenever Sylvia couldn't find the words to tell people to leave her alone, like with Meg and Archie, all without trying to tell her what she should do. Add in his way with Sophie, and a female could get used to having a male like Jake around.

Not that she should hope too much for a future with him. A lot could still happen to show they weren't really suited at all.

Her dragon huffed, but thankfully Sylvia reached Jake before she could argue with her beast about how everything could go wrong. He pulled her close, kissed her gently, and murmured, "And here I thought you'd come wearing some sort of special outfit, one you could easily toss aside to shift."

She snorted. "Not even our first shift has special

outfits. Showing someone my dragon doesn't signify any sort of life-changing event—it just is."

"It's not special, even for me?"

She touched his cheek. "Aye, of course it's a big deal with you. But seeing as Sophie could've spit up between me watching her and handing her over to Emma, I wasn't about to risk it." She leaned over to his ear and whispered, "Besides, I need to be naked to shift. And I suspect you'll like that."

He nuzzled her cheek. "As long as no one comes around when you're still naked and human, I will."

"I told you it's not a big deal for dragons. We're used to nudity. And it's a rather recent thing, history-wise, for humans to be so embarrassed by it."

"Oh, I'm sure throughout history that no one wanted to have their own special naked man or woman paraded about town, for all to see." He nibbled her earlobe and Sylvia leaned against him. "But as long as I'm the only one sharing your bed in the present, I'll learn to live with it."

She shook her head. "It's not like I have a line of suitors."

He met her gaze again. "But you should."

His words, stated so confidently, made her belly flutter. "Few are willing to not only face my in-laws but my five grown children."

"Then they're fools, all of them."

As she stared into his hazel eyes, all Sylvia could think of was how easy it would be to love this human.

And not just because it'd been so long since anyone had defended her outside of her children.

However, she wouldn't get attached. It'd been a matter of days. One argument could destroy it all, and she needed to remember that.

She lightly pushed him away. "Enough flattery for now. My inner dragon is eager to show you our dragon form, aye?"

He kissed her quickly and then gestured for her to proceed him into the landing area.

She could feel Jake's eyes on her arse as she walked, so she swayed her hips a bit more than normal.

Something she never would've done before. But the longer Jake was around, the more she wanted to be a little more teasing, or mischievous, or something other than quiet, kind Sylvia on the outskirts of everything.

It was almost like when she'd been in Glasgow.

Her dragon said, *He's good for us. I keep telling you that.*

Hush. It's time to get ready to shift.

Sylvia quickly shucked her clothes, tucked them into one of the cubbies in the rock wall, and walked toward the center.

She swore she heard a soft growl coming from Jake's direction.

Smiling, she turned to face him. And, aye, there was a mixture of heat and possessiveness in his gaze.

She shivered but quickly closed her eyes so she could concentrate and let her dragon take over.

IT TOOK everything Jake had not to run up to Sylvia and shield her naked body from anyone else's possible gaze.

While waiting for her to arrive, he'd seen a naked dragonman come out of the landing area carrying his clothes, uncaring as he nodded hello at Jake.

But with Sylvia, it was different. He didn't want to share her with anyone who walked by.

However, as she closed her eyes and her body began to change, he quickly forgot about any sort of jealousy.

Her arms and legs grew into limbs, wings grew from her back, and her face elongated into the head of a dragon. In less than a minute, a large, red dragon stood looking at him.

He'd known Sylvia could change into a dragon. Of course he had. But it was still hard to reconcile the large, sharp-toothed beast with the woman who had burst into tears a few days ago.

Still, something about her eyes held the same calm, kind look that her human form did. That snapped him out of staring, and Jake slowly walked up to her.

She wasn't the first dragon he'd seen up close—

his cousin's mate had been in his dragon form a few times when Jake had visited—but seeing Sylvia as a dragon was a long way off from a cousin-in-law he barely knew.

The large red dragon standing in front of him was the mother of his child, the woman he loved to hear laugh, the female he wanted to protect from whatever might come in the future.

And as her scales glinted faintly in the afternoon, she was magnificent.

He soon reached her, and Sylvia butted her head against his shoulder. The action made him laugh, and he finally stroked her snout.

Her scales were warm and hard, yet smooth to the touch. They were a dark red that ranged in color depending on how the light hit them.

Looking into one of her giant eyes, he said, "Is it weird for me to say you're both fierce yet pretty at the same time?"

She huffed, and he couldn't help but grin. He wasn't exactly an expert on dragon body language, but it almost seemed like a laugh.

Patting her snout, he replied, "Although I have to say we clash a bit, don't we? A red-haired man with a red dragon. What will the fashionistas say?"

The huff was stronger this time, and he laughed. "But being serious, I'll scratch behind your ear like you said to do, but then I want to touch more of you." With his cousin's mate, he'd been polite. But he wasn't going to hold back from Sylvia. Honesty was his policy with her. "Your wings look fragile yet tough. I'm curious."

She lowered her head, and he found the patch of skin behind her ear—a small strip without any scales —and he ran his nails back and forth. A humming sound rumbled from her throat, and he scratched harder.

Her dragon was definitely more catlike than dog, at least at first glance.

Once she let out a happy dragon sigh, he asked, "Can I touch your wing?"

She lowered it, and he walked over to run a finger over the thin membrane between her wing bones. While not soft, it was smooth with a slight texture, almost like textured leather.

A few beats passed before she flicked her tail. He raised his brows and met her large eye. "What, do you want me to ride your tail like some sort of mechanical bull?"

Could dragons roll their eyes? Because he swore Sylvia had.

With a snort, he went to her tail, and in the next second, he was held up into the air, high above the ground. He could see most of the clan's lands from up here, and beyond. The Scottish Highlands had a rugged kind of beauty he didn't think he'd ever get used to.

She then maneuvered her tail to place him at the

base of her neck and released him. Minding his balance, he said, "Tell me you're not going to jump into the air."

Shaking her head, she stood up on her back legs. She gestured with her forelimb into the distance.

The sun had come out briefly, and it glinted off Loch Naver nearby, a stone broch reflecting off the mostly calm water, along with some of the nearby hills.

There were also what they called forests here in Scotland—although Jake wouldn't dare, given the large swaths of trees along the west coast of the US alone—and even some ruins of abandoned cottages.

He'd seen all of these things separately, from the ground. But all together, it was breathtaking. He could only imagine how much more so it would be from the air.

All too soon, Sylvia put him back on the ground and gestured toward the side of the landing area, signaling she would shift back.

Just as she started to shrink back into her human form, another dragon appeared in the sky above the landing area. It hovered, waiting for Sylvia to finish and move to the side. Jake had no idea who the green dragon was, but Sylvia had reached his side when she murmured, "What does Arlo want?"

Arlo set his feet on the ground, landing far closer to Jake and Sylvia than he liked. Before they could move farther away, the dragon reached out, plucked

Jake up off the ground with the talons of his forearm, and jumped back into the air.

He heard Sylvia's undistinguishable voice as Arlo took him higher into the air. Looking up at the dragon, Jake shouted, "What the hell are you doing?"

But the dragonman ignored him and flapped his wings, going higher and higher into the sky.

Eventually the air became thinner, making it harder to breathe, and it got a lot colder. The last thing Jake remembered was hoping Sylvia would send help—he stood no fucking chance against a dragon carrying him in the air—before he blacked out.

Chapter Eleven

Logan Lamont approached the MacAllisters' cottage, took a deep breath, and knocked. He had no idea why Emma had asked him to come over —she'd refused to say by text—but he seemed to look for ways to torture himself. And so he'd said yes, even though he should be at home studying.

Although if all she wanted was help with her bloody geocaching adventures again, he was going to say no this time and go home. There was no way he'd stick around to watch her flirt with other males like last time.

His dragon spoke up. *If you'd stop pining for her and do something about it, everything would be fine.*

I doubt it. I tried that years ago, and it didn't work. She laughed at us, if you remember, aye? She thought it was all a lark.

But you never kissed her before. That might do it.

Logan wasn't so sure. Especially since he well knew that Emma wasn't his true mate.

He'd been halfway in love with her for years, drawn to her ability to say what she meant, laugh at herself, and secretly have a huge heart for anyone who needed help.

Not that she'd admit it, and most people didn't notice her kindness, but not long ago he'd learned of her help with some of the older clan members. Simple things like shopping, or gossiping, or just stopping round to see if anything needed doing in their houses.

Why she did it all secretly, he had no bloody idea. She hadn't even told him. No, he'd only found out about her secret volunteer work when visiting his great-aunt. She'd let it slip about how Emma MacAllister had been by again, with a new basket of shortbread, like she did every week. A little prying had revealed that the female often stopped by the elder clan members during her lunch break, but she always asked them to keep it secret. Great-Aunt Mary had said Logan was family, so surely it didn't break her promise to tell him.

But the revelation had only made him want Emma all the more.

He'd debated asking Emma about her actions in person, but the next time he'd seen her, she'd instantly blurted about some sort of treasure hunt. Even though he had studies to do—Logan was training to be a fully-fledged doctor—he'd accompanied her and the MacKay brothers on her latest little treasure-hunting adventure.

Well, not for real treasure, but apparently people around the world set up "finds" and clues via a process called geocaching. And during the excursion, he'd seen firsthand how she'd flirted with both of the Seahaven lads.

Never with Logan, however. He'd been there in case someone was injured, nothing more.

He should've said no, but he couldn't bear the thought of Emma getting hurt with no one to help her properly. Impulsive may as well be her middle name when it came to her treasure hunts.

The door opened, bringing him back to the present and revealing Emma holding her baby sister in her arms. The sight of Emma with a bairn in her arms did things to him that Logan would rather not think about.

Instead he smiled, quirked an eyebrow, and asked, "So what's this borderline emergency you texted me about?"

She pulled him inside. Once the door shut, she sighed. "I need your help with Sophie." He raised his brows. She added, "You've mentioned watching your nephew multiple times. Plus I've seen you with him at some of the smaller clan gatherings, and I figured you'd be able to tell me what to do, aye?"

Of course she wanted him to help her babysit. He was only her friend, after all.

Pushing aside his disappointment, he decided he wouldn't make this easy for her. "Why would you agree to watch her if you don't know what you're doing?"

She bit her lower lip and it took everything he had not to stare at it.

His dragon whispered, *I still say you should kiss her once and see how it goes.*

Thankfully Emma replied, "I know what I *should* be doing, and yet I'm still nervous. Mum never asks me to watch Sophie on my own. And I'm terrible with children."

He nodded toward the softly babbling bairn in her arms and said dryly, "Aye, so terrible. Why, look at how upset she is."

Emma narrowed her eyes. "Mum just left a few minutes ago, so of course Sophie's fine for the moment. But in about ten minutes, she'll start wailing for Mum. And I can never get her to quiet down."

He sighed. "Emma, you're a grown female who's lived the past three months under the same roof as wee Sophie. Surely you can handle her without me."

Emma averted her eyes to the side. "Mum didn't want to leave her with me, I could tell."

The flash of hurt in her gaze was gone before he could blink. He softened his tone a fraction. "Why would you say that?"

She looked back at him. "It's only because Jake said I should watch her that she finally agreed to it. And even then, Mum hesitated handing Sophie over. She doesn't trust me with this." Her eyes turned pleading. "Please, Logan. You're so good with your nephew. Can't you help me just this once and show me how you manage it? That way I won't let my mum down."

Emma rarely showed vulnerabilities. To most of Lochguard, she was a brash, carefree lass who had a penchant for trouble.

Yet here she was, asking him to help with her sister, afraid she'd muck it up on her own.

And bloody hell, he couldn't say no now, not for all the gold in the world.

His dragon said, *Good. I still say kiss her later and show we're more than a friend.*

He ignored his beast. "I'll help, Emma. But only help. You're going to do most of the work, aye?"

She nodded, her eyes lighting up. "Whatever you say, I promise." He raised his brows at that. She huffed. "I can follow orders when I want to, Logan."

"We'll see, lass, we'll see." He gestured toward the living area. "Let's try our best to wear her out and then maybe she'll sleep better. Where are the toys?"

And so they went and managed to keep Sophie occupied, and dry, and even fed until she finally fell asleep.

To Logan's surprise, Emma had followed his suggestions. Well, mostly.

Which was strangest of all. Emma rather liked being in charge.

Although the fact she'd been able to admit her fault showed she was finally growing up a bit, a far cry from when they were teens and she'd denied everything, no matter if she'd been in the wrong or not.

As they sat down to tea and biscuits, he thought about his dragon's words. The last time he'd asked Emma out on a date, they'd both been teenagers. Maybe she'd had a change of heart over the years.

Aye, they were friends. Rather close friends, at that. The question was whether he would risk rejection again and possibly destroy that friendship or finally find a way to move past her and remain merely as her friend.

However, before he could finish listing all the pros and cons inside his head, Emma's youngest brother, Jamie, burst into the kitchen, surprised to see Logan.

The male quickly regained his wits and said, "Uncle Arlo's taken Jake."

"What?" he and Emma said at the same time.

Jamie nodded. "It's true. I've come to help watch Sophie whilst Mum talks with Faye, Grant, and Finn."

Emma blurted, "But why would Uncle Arlo take

Jake? From what I heard, he doesn't like the human, but I didn't think he'd resort to something like that."

Jamie's face turned grim. "No, he doesn't like the human. He snatched him in his dragon form and flew away."

Logan blinked at that. It was against clan rules to merely pick someone up and fly away without their consent, no matter if they were human or dragon.

Not to mention if the DDA got word of it, Arlo MacAllister would most likely end up in jail.

Sophie started crying from upstairs, and Logan motioned for Emma and Jamie to stay. "I'll help with her until things calm down. Finish telling Emma the details."

Emma gave him a look of gratitude before he went upstairs to check on the bairn.

Any thoughts of trying to be more than Emma's friend fled his mind. Her family was about to go through hell and back, and she'd probably need him to lean on.

And as he went about calming Sophie, Logan decided it'd have to be enough.

For now.

Chapter Twelve

The sight of Arlo flying away with Jake in his talons was something Sylvia wouldn't ever forget.

Especially as he flew higher and higher into the atmosphere.

The thought of Arlo doing something rash, like dropping Jake, snapped her out of her shock. If there was to be any chance Jake survived, he needed her. And since she knew she couldn't chase Arlo and catch up with him, let alone know how to deal with him if she did, she needed the clan's help.

Sylvia quickly threw on her clothes and raced toward the Protector's main building, ignoring anyone along the way, doing her best to focus on the goal of getting help for Jake. Now wasn't the time for worries or doubts.

When she finally burst through the doors, she spotted Iris Mahajan, one of the female Protectors—those in charge of Lochguard's security—and blurted, "Arlo's taken Jake. He grabbed him and flew away."

Iris closed the distance between them. "Which way did he go?"

"To the east."

The dragonwoman nodded. "I'll see if I can catch him." She looked at the person sitting at the front desk. "Get Sylvia to Faye and Grant."

In the next second, Iris was gone and Sylvia was being led down the hall to one of the meeting rooms. The young dragon male said, "Just one second," and ran out of the room.

Sylvia couldn't sit and instead paced the room. Why the bloody hell would Arlo steal Jake like that? Aye, Jake had stood up to the male, but she didn't think Arlo would break clan rules to teach Jake some sort of lesson.

Would he?

She knew Arlo the least of all of the MacAllister in-laws, despite the fact he was the first she'd ever met as a teen, even before Arthur. But to be honest, she'd never wanted to know him better after Cat and Connor had told her about the male threatening to take away her children.

Although it still didn't make sense for Arlo to risk

everything—his place in the clan, his business, even his family—to punish one human. So why had he done it?

Her dragon spoke up. *Faye and Grant will figure it out. You just have to trust them.*

Before she could reply, Faye and Grant burst into the room. Considering Faye was sans daughter— Faye was almost always carrying her daughter around—they were both ready to act at a moment's notice.

Grant spoke first. "Arlo took Jake?"

She nodded and briefly recapped what had happened before asking, "But why?"

Faye frowned. "I don't know. He hasn't done anything suspicious we can tell in recent years. We've kept a close eye on everyone since Finn kicked out all the clan members who refused to accept him as leader, but Arlo never even came up on our radar for a minor infraction."

Several years ago, a number of clan members had betrayed Finn, and he'd sent the disloyal ones packing. Some said they lived with other clan-less dragon-shifters somewhere in Scotland. Sylvia hadn't thought much about it since it'd happened.

Grant grunted. "Iris is trying to see if she can track him down, and others are talking to those close to Arlo." He paused and looked at Faye. Once the dragonwoman nodded, he added, "And we have someone keeping an eye on the rogue dragon-shifters. If Arlo shows up there, we'll know soon after."

Sylvia bit her lip. "So there's nothing else we can do?"

Faye took her hand and squeezed. "We're doing all we can, but the best thing for you is to go home and take care of Sophie."

Sylvia wasn't a Protector, or spy, or trained in any sort of way that could help Faye, Grant, and the others.

And yet, she hated being so useless.

Her dragon spoke up. *We're not useless. Sophie needs us. The best thing we can do is ensure she's well and happy for when her dad returns.*

If he returned was left unsaid.

She was just about to demand that Faye and Grant keep her updated when her son Connor burst through the door. "Is it true? Did Arlo take Jake?"

She nodded. "Aye, although I wish I knew why." Connor hesitated a second and took a step toward her eldest son. "What is it? Do you know something?"

"Maybe."

Grant crossed his arms over his chest. "Then tell us, lad."

Connor stood tall as he replied, "Well, it was over a decade ago now, aye? But right after Dad was murdered, and Mum was still grieving hard, Uncle Arlo came over and threatened to take us kids away."

Sylvia frowned. "Aye, but what does that have to do with anything?"

"There's a part of his demand that Cat and I didn't tell you." She raised her brows, and her son continued, "He said if you mated him, he'd take care of us all. That was the only way to ensure we could all stay together."

She blinked. "What? Why would he demand that? Arthur had only been dead for weeks at that point."

Connor shrugged. "I don't know why exactly. But he said something about how you should've always been his, and he was the only one who could save you. Cat and I were angry at him wanting to replace Dad so soon. And to not upset you further, we decided to keep it secret. But I thought it might be important now."

A feeling of dread grew in the pit of her stomach, one she didn't want to think about but oddly made sense. Before she could change her mind, she blurted, "Did he have something to do with Arthur's death?"

Connor's eyes widened. "What are you talking about?"

Sylvia sank into a chair before her knees gave out, everything starting to make a horrible, awful kind of sense.

Faye squeezed her shoulder and said softly, "Tell us whatever it is you're thinking, Sylvia."

For a second, she couldn't make her voice work.

Then her dragon said, *Maybe it's not true, but they need to know all the facts.*

Taking a deep breath, Sylvia said, "Arlo was the first MacAllister brother to try to woo me. He was a lot older than me, and one short conversation about how lucky I'd be to be courted by him when so many others were trying to catch his eye was all it took for my gut and mind to refuse him." She swallowed. "He didn't take it well."

The disbelief and anger in Arlo's eyes, especially to a sixteen-year-old girl, had frightened her.

Until Arthur had shown up.

She continued, "Arthur heard his brother yelling and came to defend me. He managed to chase Arlo away and ensured I was all right. Despite it all, he somehow made me laugh and feel safe." She picked at the hem of her top. "And we went on from there." She met each of the three people's gazes in the room in turn. "Arlo was always grumpy after Arthur and I mated, but I figured he'd accepted it. Especially as the years went on and he became nicer to me." Emotion choked her throat but she pushed on. "He was the first to comfort me when Arthur was merely missing." She shook her head. "But could it be possible? If, mere weeks after Arthur's death, Arlo said I should've been his, then could he have helped orchestrate Arthur's death to get me?"

Grant answered, "I don't know. The case was

before my time, but we're going to look into it. For now, in addition to taking care of Sophie, I need you to be ready in case we need you."

She met his gaze again. "Need me? For what?"

Grant's expression turned grim. "It'll be a last resort, aye? But we might need you as bait or to talk with Arlo. If his obsession is still there, then my guess is that he won't kill Jake but barter his life to get you."

The thought of Arlo even touching her made her shiver. The only good to come from his possible obsession was that there was still a small chance Jake was alive.

Connor started to protest but Sylvia cut him off. "Aye, whatever you need. I'll do it."

Faye nodded. "Then you'd best go home and rest as best you can, and make arrangements in case you need to leave Sophie for a bit."

Connor spoke up. "Don't worry, Mum. Me and the others can help with Sophie."

She smiled at her son. "Thanks, Connor."

Faye spoke again. "However, before you two leave, tell us everything you can about Arlo MacAllister. And don't leave anything out."

As they did so, Sylvia hoped with her entire being that she was wrong about Arlo's motivations.

And yet, the more she thought about it, the more she started to think her gut was right.

At every chance encounter since she and the

MacAllisters had reconciled, he'd watched her closely. She'd always thought it was because he was looking for a chance to show she was unfit, as if he was out to prove she wasn't a good mother.

But maybe it'd been more.

And all because she'd refused him more than twenty years ago.

Regardless of Arlo's true motivations, Sylvia was going to be strong this time. If she had to corner the MacAllisters herself to demand answers, she'd do it.

Jake, Sophie, and any hint of happiness in her future depended on it.

Too long Sylvia had let others step in to defend her, or help her, or coax her to do what needed to be done. But no longer. It was her time to shine and prove to herself and everyone else what she was made of.

So she finished with Faye and Grant and went home to her daughter. She'd have to arrange for her children to help her, but she wouldn't hesitate to ask this time. Only then could she talk to the one person who might know more about Arlo's goal—his brother Seamus. Of anyone, he was the one who'd tell her the truth. After all, there wasn't any love lost between the two brothers. They rarely saw eye to eye on anything.

The only question was whether Seamus would betray his brother to help his sister-in-law.

Her dragon grunted. *We won't know until we try.*

Aye, I know. So let's get Sophie sorted and find him.

A strength and determination she'd never felt before coursed through her. Even if it'd been a short time they'd been together, Jake was hers.

And a dragon always protected what was theirs.

Chapter Thirteen

Sylvia had first tried Seamus's home. However, she learned he wasn't there but at his office situated near the clan's central area.

As she marched toward the building, Sylvia did her best to keep herself calm. Part of her wanted to lash out at Seamus for possibly deceiving her and supporting Arlo. And yet another part of her was sad at the thought of his betrayal.

After Arthur's death, she'd always thought Seamus her best ally from among all the MacAllisters. He'd been the only one to ask—and really meant it—about how she was doing instead of merely trying to determine how the children were faring.

Her dragon spoke up. *Find out the truth from Seamus first. I find it hard to believe a solicitor would willingly engage in something illegal. Especially with Arlo, given the past between the two brothers.*

I wish it were that simple. However, the MacAllisters are close, despite what happened with that female. You know that.

Regardless, talk with him first. Maybe Seamus is innocent in all this and can help us.

All she could do was hope.

Sylvia reached the offices used by Lochguard's two lawyers and did her best to smile at the assistant manning the front desk. Within a few minutes, Sylvia was inside a conference room, pacing and doing her best to keep her fear tamped down.

Because all it would take was for Arlo to drop Jake and her human would be gone forever.

Sophie would lose her father. And Sylvia would lose any chance at finding happiness with another male.

No. Jake needed her to keep her head and get to the bottom of everything, to help him any way she could. And for once, Sylvia was going to follow through. She could worry about fear, grief, and the ensuing depression later, if it came to that. For now, she held out hope.

A knock on the door followed by Seamus entering the room, his dark brown hair streaked with gray and his brows knitted together. "What's wrong, Sylvia? If it's about my dad, I'm doing my best to keep him away. But he's rather good at sneaking around and causing trouble."

She stopped pacing and stated, "I'm not here about Archie. I'm here about Arlo."

His brows raised. "What's my brother done now?"

She searched his eyes, trying to determine if Seamus was playacting or truly surprised. "You don't know? Because if you do, you need to tell me. I'm sure having a murderer in your family wouldn't be good for business, aye?"

"Murderer?" Seamus took a step toward her. "What are you talking about?"

Could it be true? Did Seamus not know?

"Don't play with me, Seamus. Jake's life is at risk."

He reached out as if to touch her arm but then stopped himself. "I swear I know nothing about what Arlo's done. I can't help you if you don't tell me what's going on."

She bit her lip a second before blurting, "He snatched Jake and flew away. I think he might want to kill him."

Seamus's gaze turned unreadable. "He's a fool, aye, but that big of one?"

"I don't have time to debate how much of a fool your brother is. Has Arlo acted out of the ordinary lately?" She wasn't ready to reveal her suspicions to Seamus, not until she could better judge whose side he was on. "Anything that could tell us why he'd take Jake?"

For a beat, she didn't think he'd answer. But

finally Seamus ran a hand through his hair and said, "Arlo has been acting strange lately, aye, and more secretive than normal. However, he usually acts that way whenever one of his lovers breaks up with him. I figured that was the case again. But kidnapping? Why would he do that?"

She was starting to think Seamus didn't know about Arlo's threats and words to her children right after Arthur had died.

Regardless, she pushed aside the hope he was innocent to focus on getting more information. "No one truly knows why he did it except for Arlo. But I need to know—is there somewhere he could've taken Jake? I know the two of you aren't close since, well, that female. But he is your brother. Maybe he could've said something at some point?"

Seamus's lips thinned at the mention of the female Arlo had deliberately seduced away from him. It may have happened years ago, but Sylvia had always suspected the female had been Seamus's true mate and Arlo had done it on purpose.

Arlo MacAllister didn't like to lose. She'd always known that, but only recently had she started to understand how far he might go to win.

However, she didn't much care about the two brothers' relationship, only what Seamus might know to help bring back Jake.

The dragonman finally blew out a breath. "His last lover liked extreme role-playing. Arlo constantly bragged about it to me and my cousins. He mentioned how he liked to pretend to imprison her somewhere in the Orkneys and have her 'convince' him to free her. But I don't know any more than that. I vow it."

Dragon-shifters took vows rather seriously. A few might break them without thinking, but her gut said Seamus wasn't one of them.

And not just because she'd seen him defend countless members of her clan over the years against false human-made accusations either.

She nodded, but Seamus continued before she could reply. "I swear I had nothing to do with this, Sylvia. I know you have no reason to trust me, but I hold no grudge against humans or the fact you fancy one. Aye, I've dealt with some horrid ones over the years in my profession, but you know Lacey was human too."

Lacey had been the female Arlo had stolen away from him more than twenty years ago. By the use of past tense, Sylvia wondered if she'd died.

Maybe it was why he'd remained unattached all these years. Once she had Jake back safe and sound, Sylvia was going to try and better know Seamus. She knew what it was to lose someone and be lonely. And a friend who understood that could help more than he'd probably ever realize.

But Jake was her priority for now. Searching Seamus's gaze, she finally nodded. "I appreciate the information, but the bigger question is—will you side with Arlo if he's caught? Because he's going to be charged, you know it. Since a human is involved, both Finn and the DDA will deal with him."

Seamus stood a little taller. "I believe in the law. I won't simply look the other way because Arlo and I share blood. He's been bringing trouble to himself nearly his whole life. I once tried to help him, back before he betrayed me, but I gave up on him years ago and I've merely tolerated him for my dad's sake. Anything you and Jake need, just ask and I'll do my best to help."

Both woman and beast heard the truth to his words.

Sylvia reached out and squeezed his fingers. "Thank you, Seamus. Will you come with me to talk to Faye and Grant? They might have more questions about Arlo that you can answer."

"Aye, of course."

As the two of them headed toward the main Protector building, a small flicker of hope burned in her chest. The Orkney Islands were an archipelago, aye. But it was somewhere to begin a search.

And that was a start.

A MIXTURE of sounds slowly nudged Jake into consciousness. The crash of waves, the cries of a few birds, and gusts of strong wind.

The scent of brine brought him even more awake, until he blinked his eyes open.

Light filtered in from a tiny window, letting him see where he was. The walls were made of stone, the floor was only dirt, and the window didn't have any glass in it.

There was a solid wooden door, though, but it looked sturdier than the rest of the place, and he doubted it could easily be forced open.

Arlo was nowhere to be seen, so Jake took the chance to rise to his feet. After a moment of unsteadiness, he walked to the window. It was barely big enough for his head to poke through, but he didn't need to do that to see a vast, open space of water with some jagged peaks in the distance.

Craning his head, he looked either way and found a similar sight or water and land in the distance. Even without being able to see the fourth side of his prison, he guessed he was on some sort of island.

And since he was in Scotland, it could be any number of them. Up north were a ton of uninhabited islands, for starters. Although his report from his cousin hadn't mentioned the dragon-shifters having any clans living on the islands, though, so probably no one on Lochguard could guess he'd been taken here.

Turning back toward the room, he rubbed his face and tried to wake himself up a little more. His brain was foggy, as if it didn't want to work right. And even if Arlo could easily kill him without thought when he returned, Jake was determined to find out as much as he could about his prison so he could form a few plans. He didn't doubt Sylvia would get him some help.

If the Lochguard dragons did find him— although he wasn't 100 percent confident they would —he wanted to avoid being a burden and help in any way he could.

Although as he walked around the one-room cottage, studying it, the only thing he noticed was how some of the stones must've shifted over time since there were large gaps in parts of the walls.

Surveying the room again, his thoughts drifted back to Arlo. Jake didn't really understand *why* the dragonman had taken him. Simply because Jake had stood up to him? Or was there something more? Hatred had flashed briefly in the dragonman's eyes when they'd first met, not that he'd understood why.

As far as Jake knew, Lochguard accepted humans on their lands. His cousin's report had said as much.

Something else was up; it had to be.

Needing to focus on something, anything, to avoid going down the path of what-ifs, he walked back to the biggest gap in the wall. It was near the top, not far from the rotted thatch ceiling.

If he could push out one or two of the stones, then he might be able to create a handhold to try and find a weak spot to knock down some of the thatch. If he did that, he might be able to escape via the roof.

Or at least look out to see all of his surroundings to better see where he was.

He'd barely spent any time at all trying to wiggle a stone loose when something splashed loudly in the water nearby. Through the window, he saw the shape of a green dragon.

Arlo was back.

Jake quickly moved to a different part of the room, sat against the wall, and pretended to look weaker than he was.

A beat later, the door banged open, revealing Arlo in his naked human form. "You're awake. Good."

He strode inside, tugging a short, bound, and gagged woman behind him, one with black hair and golden skin. Jake had no idea who she was, but the look of resignation in her dark brown eyes made him wonder what the hell was going on.

Arlo stopped several feet away, tossed a pair of handcuffs toward Jake, and then tugged the woman against his front, extending a talon to her neck.

And still the woman merely looked resigned to her fate before she shut her eyes.

Arlo growled, "Put on the handcuffs or I'll slit her throat." As if making a point, he pressed a fraction, and a drop of blood rolled down the woman's neck.

Jake debated whether Arlo was bluffing or not when the dragonman pressed even harder against the woman's throat and she cried out as best as she could through her gag.

Just as he thought about reaching for the cuffs, the woman opened her eyes again. This time, they were full of determination. She winked at Jake, then stepped on Arlo's insole. His talon moved a fraction away. She ducked down, elbowed him in the stomach, and then turned to kick him in the balls as the bindings around her wrists fell away.

In the next instant, she had him on his stomach, her arm wrapped around his neck. She didn't say a word, but Arlo's body soon went slack. Only then did she stand up, tug off the gag, and extracted a capped syringe from between her breasts. As she stuck it into Arlo's bicep, she finally spoke, her accent some sort of English one. "Hand me the cuffs."

Jake did as she asked, still trying to figure out what the hell was going on.

However, given how the woman had just taken out a dragon-shifter despite having a talon to her throat, he decided to be cautious. Demanding anything wouldn't help. No, she'd have to tell him on her own terms.

Once Arlo was restrained, she finally stood, rolled her shoulders, and faced him. "Right, then. Dealing with him is the easy part. Now we just have to survive the bloody cold until Antony or his cohorts arrives."

Sensing she wasn't about to disarm him the same way as Arlo, he asked, "Who're you?"

"You can call me Trina for now. And don't ask how I came to be here because I can't tell you. Not yet." She patted down Arlo until she found his cell phone. "No service, as I thought. Bloody islands. But no matter, they'll find us soon enough. Come with me. I saw some driftwood that might be dry enough to make a fire. We'll start there."

She exited the room and he could do nothing but follow the strange yet fascinating woman who took down a dragon-shifter without so much as breaking a sweat. "But what about Arlo?"

Trina waved a hand in dismissal. "Thanks to the shot I gave him, his dragon will be silent for days. So don't worry about him. He can't shift and he won't be able to break those cuffs either."

He frowned. "Do you really expect me not to ask who you really are?"

She shrugged. "You can try. But trust me, I can resist."

And given her display earlier, he didn't doubt it.

Still, Jake kept a wary distance from the woman

as they gathered wood for a fire. And once they went back to the small cottage, cleared out the dilapidated chimney, and were reasonably warm, the woman further tied up Arlo and tossed him into a corner.

She said nothing, ignoring Jake and only checking the window occasionally.

Now he had no fucking idea what Arlo had been up to. And given what the woman said about not saying anything, all he could do was come up with theories for the current situation.

Just what had Arlo gotten himself involved in? And what would happen to Jake?

Chapter Fourteen

Iris Mahajan had barely managed to tug on the loose dress she'd carried with her in her dragon form before dashing toward the cottage at the edge of the village where one of her contacts lived.

It'd been a slow day, visiting those she paid to keep her informed of any dragon sightings. Usually she used the humans to keep tabs on the rogue dragon-shifters who moved around parts of Scotland at times, but the network had proved useful for tracking down Arlo as well.

Especially since she hadn't been able to find Arlo on her own—he'd be long gone by the time she'd launched herself into the air back on Lochguard—it had been her last resort to try and find him the hard way. It'd taken five visits before she'd had her first reported sighting. But now she was growing nearer the northeastern part of Sutherland, which worried her. Because if Arlo went to any of the isles further north, she'd lose track of him.

Which would mean failure.

Her dragon spoke up. *Even if we lose his trail now, narrowing it down to the isles will help the others in planning their search.*

Aye, I know. I still don't like it, though. Arlo should be easier to find than this since he's never served with the military or had any sort of specialized training.

People become unpredictable when they're frantic to escape.

She mentally sighed. *I just wish I'd noticed something was off about him earlier.*

Just because you couldn't predict Arlo's behavior doesn't mean we failed.

Iris wished she could agree. But she prided herself on being able to read people well, to the point she had been in charge of watching for any more troublemakers or traitors since Finn banished the disloyal clan members years ago.

Thankfully she reached the cottage of Katrina Lau, a young human widow who was one of her more recently recruited informants, and Iris easily pushed everything else aside to focus on her task.

Ensuring no one else was around, she knocked on the front door in a particular rhythm and then darted back to the hedges. She heard the click of the back door being unlocked, and Iris rushed toward it, turned the doorknob, and entered.

She hated being so dramatic, but not everyone

liked dragon-shifters in this wee village. And she preferred being careful to risking their ire or causing an unnecessary scene.

She headed to the living room where the curtains were drawn, as usual for their meetings, but instead of Katrina, there was a tall, pale man dressed in an unremarkable suit. His light brown hair was graying at the temples, and his brown eyes seemed somewhat familiar despite the fact she'd never seen this male before in her life. With a hand behind her back, she extended a talon as a precaution and demanded, "Who the bloody hell are you?"

His accent said he was from somewhere near London. "You may call me Antony. And there's no need to stab me, dragonwoman. Retract your talon."

Iris knew how to keep her face impassive, but she had to admit she was a wee bit impressed he'd guessed what she was hiding behind her back.

Still, she kept her talon at the ready. "Tell me, where's the woman who owns this cottage?"

He shrugged and picked some imaginary lint off his sleeve, as if to prove he wasn't afraid of her. Or, maybe even she bored him with her threats.

However, Iris had long ago learned that males underestimated her. It almost always worked to her advantage.

She was tempted to show him the error of his ways, but she wanted information more than a fight. "Well? Where is she?"

His gaze met hers, and he merely raised an eyebrow. "Your talon is still out. I'll wait until you put it away."

She barely resisted clenching her jaw at his words, as if she'd merely follow his order because he wanted it.

However, her dragon snorted and spoke up. *I'm not sure why, but I sort of like him.*

He could've kidnapped Trina, for all we know. So behave.

Her beast sniffed. *Of course I will. It doesn't mean I can't look.*

Iris ignored his tall, lean body and focused solely on his eyes. "First, take off your jacket and show me you aren't carrying any weapons."

He shrugged it off and murmured, "I don't need to carry anything to still have a weapon."

With most males, she'd dismiss it as bragging. But something about the way he flexed his fingers and pierced her with his intense gaze told her he was speaking the truth.

Still, he was human, that much she could tell by his scent. It would take a lot for him to best her in a fight, even if she were a female dragon-shifter.

Once he finished turning around to show no weapons, she sheathed her talon and showed both her hands. "Aye, well, we're both harmless now. So answer my question."

"You're far from harmless, my dear."

She usually hated when males used fake

endearments with her, as if trying to say she was somehow lesser because of her gender. And yet, the way this human said it held a combination of power and praise that made her wonder who the hell he truly was.

Not that she would waste time thinking about it right now.

So Iris merely raised her brows and waited to see if he'd answer her question. With a snort, Antony finally replied, "Trina is alive and well, I promise you that. Although she's no widow, and she works for me. For months, we've been trying to pin down the Scottish dragon-shifter selling dragon's blood on the black market. We recently determined it was Arlo MacAllister, and thanks to Trina, we have proof."

Despite her best efforts to remain unaffected, she did blink at that information. "What?"

His eyes turned smug. "Don't look so surprised. I've heard you're good, but we're better. Don't fret about us deceiving you."

For a beat, every hard-earned achievement she'd made in both the British Army and with the Protectors faded away. This human and the female one had discovered Arlo's crimes—if they were true —without her even catching on to it.

Maybe Iris wasn't as good as she thought she was.

Her dragon growled. *We are. Think of all the missing persons we've tracked down, the warnings we gave Finn because of information we unearthed. We're bloody good. This human male is a puzzle, but don't let him get to you.*

Her beast was right, of course. Iris did a bloody good job helping her clan. And only a fool would think they could be invincible and never make a mistake.

She'd just have to be more careful in the future and learn from this one.

Iris took a step toward him, not allowing his greater height to intimidate her one bit. "If you're as good as you say you are, then you know why I'm here, and it has nothing to do with dragon's blood or the black market. Where's Arlo MacAllister?"

He took a step closer, and Iris ignored the heat rolling off his body. He may be older than her by more than a decade—probably in his late forties—but it didn't make him any less dangerous.

Or attractive.

No. She wouldn't allow a little attraction to deter her or make her lose focus.

He finally answered, "In order for me to share information about Arlo MacAllister, I need you to vow to help me."

She frowned. "Help you with what?"

Antony took another step closer, but Iris had steeled herself against his heat and scent and didn't react as he said, "Why, with transportation, of course. I need you to fly me to where Arlo, Jake Swift, and Trina are."

The fact he knew about Jake made her more wary than trusting. "I won't leave here without calling my superiors."

"Ah, yes. I forgot about those. I rarely answer to anyone any longer. But the best you can do is send one text message, stating you'll meet them and one of my men along the shores of the Loch of Wester."

She raised her brows. "And you expect me to just jump and do your bidding without question? For all I know, it could be a trap."

Antony merely smiled. "Would it help to know we have a friend in common?"

That was one of the last things she'd expected him to claim. She blurted, "Who the bloody hell would that be? You don't strike me as someone who has time for friends."

He shrugged. "True. But I make time for my brother."

And damn it, she couldn't stop her curiosity from demanding, "And who's your brother?"

"Dr. Maximilian Holbrook."

Max was a somewhat annoying human archaeologist who often came to Lochguard and persuaded Finn to have them escort him to one dig site or another.

As he was talkative, easily distracted, and a wee bit reckless, Max was the complete opposite of the male in front of her. "I don't believe you. I'm sure you did some research and found some name to toss my way, to try and gain my trust."

He shrugged, as if he hadn't expected any other reaction. "Let me call him, shall I?" Before she could say anything else, Antony took out his mobile phone, dialed, and set it to loudspeaker.

A male voice answered. "Hello?"

"Max, are you busy?"

"I'm always busy, Tony. I'm trying to outsmart this new bloody dragon archaeologist. She thinks she can steal my site from me, but I won't let her."

For a second, Iris's heart skipped a beat. *No.* It couldn't be.

But Antony spoke again before she could say a word. "Shall I come down and sort it out for you? You're my brother, after all."

The male grunted on the other side of the line. "Of course not. I can handle this myself. She's not as clever as she thinks she is. She's playing right into my hands."

As Iris's heart pounded inside her chest, she didn't hear the rest of Max's words.

The male on the other side of the line was undeniably Dr. Maximilian Holbrook. She'd know that voice anywhere. She'd had to babysit him often enough over the years, and one of his habits was to chatter endlessly about his work. She could pick out his voice in her sleep.

And she now knew why the human's eyes looked

familiar to her—they were the same shape and shade as Max's. Similar and yet so different at the same time.

Antony grinned at her as he finally said goodbye to his brother and put away his phone. "Max has mentioned you more than once, Iris Mahajan. He seems to like you. It'd hurt him to hurt you, and I wouldn't do that to my baby brother. So put aside your mistrust for a moment, let's bring everyone back, and then you can go back to being as wary of me for as long as you like."

Staring at the human male, Iris wanted to pinch herself to find it was all some sort of weird dream.

But she was fully awake, and it seemed she'd landed in the middle of some sort of spy movie. Because Antony was either that or some sort of secretive mercenary.

Which was why she wasn't going to just instantly trust him because he was Max's brother. Siblings betrayed siblings sometimes, as she'd witnessed firsthand when the disgruntled dragon-shifters had left Lochguard a few years ago. "First, give me one bit of information on good faith. Where's Jake?"

She studied him as he stated, "Somewhere in the Orkney Islands."

He didn't seem to display any signs of deceit—no elevated heart rate, or looking away, or fidgeting. True, he could merely be good at hiding his emotions.

Her dragon spoke up. *I don't think he's lying about that either. And dragons are better at noticing it most of the time.*

Most, but not always.

Send word back to Grant and then see where he takes us. Despite what he can do on the ground, we'll have the advantage in the air.

Not that she'd drop him, for Max's sake. Even if the human male could be a wee bit irritating, Iris had no desire to hurt Max willingly.

And for all she knew, he was close to his brother.

However, she'd still keep her eye on Antony, of course. But she owed it to Sylvia and her clan to at least follow this lead.

She took out her mobile phone. "Is there anything I can't say in my message?"

"Don't mention my name or my relation to Max. Otherwise, say what you wish."

Iris quickly typed out a message to one of her bosses, Grant, and then put her phone away. She went to the back door, opened it, and strode out. She didn't stop until she was near where she'd landed. "If I so much as see a weapon when we're in the air, I'll drop you without a thought. You're forewarned."

The bastard smirked. "Noted."

"Now, tell me where we're going."

He took out some sort of device and then gave her directions before saying, "I'll direct you in more detail when we're close. I won't wave a weapon, but I'll tap your talon."

"Fine. Now, turn around."

He raised a brow at her tone but ignored it to say, "And one more thing—I won't be going back with you, but you'll need to meet with my man at the lake and tell him my location. Don't follow through with my order, and it won't be pretty, later on, I promise you."

The bastard was a bit dramatic for her liking. She rolled her eyes before barking again, "Aye. Now, turn around."

He finally did as she asked. Iris quickly retrieved her satchel, stuffed her dress into it, and shifted.

Before she knew it, she was in the air with Antony gripped in one of her forelimbs, doing her best not to look down at the male and wish she knew more about him.

Chapter Fifteen

Jake had been staring into the fire for hours, wondering about how worried Sylvia had to be, when something splashed along the shore. Trina moved toward the door and he followed. Outside, standing in the shallow water was a purple dragon, and a few feet up the shore where it was dry was a pale man, not much older than him, dressed in a suit.

The man approached him, shared a glance with Trina—they knew each other, obviously—and then said, "We're here to take you back to the mainland, Jake." He frowned at the man knowing his name, but he continued before Jake could say anything, waving at the dragon as he did so. "This is Iris Mahajan, one of Lochguard's Protectors. She can waste time shifting back to tell you, or you can simply go with her and get back to Lochguard sooner."

The unknown male apparently knew a hell of a lot about Jake, which made him wonder how. Especially since Trina hadn't made any calls or used anything that could send a message, as far as he could tell.

Maybe they'd been watching him. But why? Did the British government keep tabs on all foreigners who set foot on a dragon clan's land? That was the only reason he could think of for being watched.

Jake quickly switched his focus to the purple dragon. Her name rang a bell. Then he remembered —he'd met her during one of his visits to Finn's office, albeit in her human form.

Glancing back to the man, he said, "Frankly, I don't know you. And seeing as I've already been kidnapped by one dragon-shifter today, I'd rather talk to Iris and confirm both her identity and your story before I go anywhere."

The man merely raised a brow. "Have it your way." He glanced at Trina, and then they headed into the dilapidated cottage.

The dragon began to shrink into her human form, and Jake turned around. He knew that dragon-shifters didn't care about nudity, but it still seemed weird to him to openly see another naked woman when all he wanted was to see Sylvia again.

Iris's voice filled the air. "Turn around, Jake."

He did and was grateful to see it was indeed the dark-haired, brown-skinned dragonwoman he'd met before. And she wore some sort of loose dress, as if knowing he was uncomfortable with her nudity.

Once they were close enough for whispering, he asked, "Who are these people?"

She shook her head. "I only know some of it. But I'd rather get going before the male changes his mind. We have a rendezvous point where my clan members should be waiting, along with some bloke of Antony's I have to pass information onto."

"Do you trust them? I get the feeling they're some sort of secret agents or something."

Iris shrugged. "I wouldn't say I trust them. But for this one instance, I think Antony and his female are helping us. I can't speak for the future though, aye?"

Even though Jake didn't know Iris well, Finn trusted her implicitly and said Jake could rely on her. And so far, Finn hadn't given Jake any reason not to believe him. "And what about Arlo?"

She raised her dark brows. "He's here?"

He nodded, explained what had happened, and then Iris replied, "Aye, well, stay here a second and I'll see what they're doing with him now."

"I can't let you go in there alone."

Iris smiled at him. "I can take care of myself, Jake. And whilst I know Antony shouldn't hurt me, I can't say the same about you. So stay put."

He hated being so useless, but Jake knew his strengths and faults, and taking on skilled agents, or whatever they were, wasn't his forte. So he nodded and Iris went in alone.

Tapping his hand against his thigh, he was eager to leave. He yearned to hold his daughter in his arms and reassure her he hadn't left her on purpose. Even if she couldn't understand, it would make him feel better.

Finally Iris returned wearing a scowl. Before he could ask, she growled, "They're going to take him in custody. And apparently there will be a report by tomorrow on Finn's desk, detailing all of his crimes."

Jake wanted to know more, such as why the damn dragonman had taken him in the first place.

As if Iris could read his thoughts, her expression softened a fraction. "Finn will make sure to find out why he snatched you and see if any others wish you harm. He didn't tolerate threats to him or his clan before, and Finn won't sit idly by now, either."

Jake was about to say he wasn't part of Lochguard, but held his tongue. He'd rather leave this place and be that much closer to seeing his two ladies and holding them close.

With a nod, Jake turned back around. "Okay. Then shift and let's get the hell out of here."

Iris snorted but went back into the water along the shore. Once she tapped his shoulder with a talon, he faced her again. And before he knew it, Jake was back up in the fucking air, yet again hoping a dragon wouldn't drop him.

Chapter Sixteen

F inn had sent Sylvia home, saying there was nothing else she could do.

Which was why the next morning she lay on her bed, her daughter sleeping next to her, and tried her best not to think of every little thing that could've gone wrong.

Aye, Finn, Faye, and Grant had appreciated her questioning Seamus, but it didn't seem nearly enough.

And given the last time she'd had to wait and see what had happened to the male she cared for, Sylvia didn't like to think of how they could bring her bad news this time too.

Her dragon said softly, *Last time we had no idea Arthur was in so much danger. But both Lochguard and the DDA are working to find Jake. This time will be different.*

She wanted to believe it. She truly did.

However, she was also steeling herself for the worst, in case she needed to be strong for her daughter.

She must've finally dozed off because Connor's loud voice jolted her awake. "Mum! They've found him."

Sylvia sat up carefully, but Sophie had woken up too and squirmed. Quickly picking her bairn up, she focused on Connor. "Well, don't stand there. Tell me what happened, lad."

Connor shrugged. "I don't know any of the details. However, he's alive. That's all Grant would say. But Finn wants to see you." He held out his arms. "I can take Sophie."

Her daughter moved her lips, signaling she was hungry. She yearned to hear news of Jake, but if Grant said Jake was alive, she had to believe her human wasn't in any immediate danger of dying. "Let me feed her first, just in case I have to be away all day."

Connor nodded. "I need to call and ensure someone else can cook today at the restaurant. I'll be downstairs."

As Sylvia fed her daughter, she did her best to wonder why Finn wanted to see her. Maybe Jake had been hurt and couldn't come to see her himself?

Or maybe Finn would say Jake needed to mate her to stay.

The thought should scare her, given that they

hadn't truly known each other long. But having Jake ripped from her side had made her realize a few things.

The most important being that she'd never felt as safe and cared for—not to mentioned desired—as she had with Jake since her late mate had died.

And even if it didn't work out between them, at least she and Jake could raise Sophie together. She gently stroked her daughter's cheek. She may be a babe, but Sylvia knew Sophie would want her father close by, if given the choice.

Her beast spoke up. *Would that be enough, though? To merely raise her together?*

One step at a time, dragon. That's all I can handle right now.

Once Sophie was fed and changed, she kissed her daughter's cheek, handed her over to Connor, and raced to Finn's place.

Finn's mate, Arabella, showed her in. But when Sylvia stepped into Finn's office, her heart sank. Jake wasn't there. "Is he hurt?"

Her clan leader shook his head, his expression unreadable. "No, he's alive and well with just a few bruises. Sit down, Sylvia. We need to chat."

Finn usually had a smile or a joke. The fact he didn't told her things weren't good.

As soon as she sat in the chair in front of his desk, Finn spoke again. "I received a short report this morning from the DDA about Arlo. Apparently, he was selling dragon blood illegally. And as damning as that is, in the end, it helped them locate Jake rather quickly."

She pushed aside her shock at what else Arlo had been up to. "What about Jake?"

"I'm getting to that." She opened her mouth to tell him to hurry up, but Finn beat her to it. "Between hacking Arlo's computer and this short report I received this morning from the DDA, it appears he's been obsessed with you for some time. There were numerous plans to kidnap you and flee to the continent. It was almost as if he was thinking of every sort of plan he could, until he found one that would work."

She gripped the arms of the chair tightly. "After learning a few things, I suspected yesterday he might've felt that way."

"Aye, well, it seems he has some contacts within the rogue dragon-shifters hiding out somewhere in Scotland. Except we don't know who they are exactly, or if he has others he's working with inside of Lochguard. Whilst he was open about plans to get you, he never mentioned names beyond his and yours."

Her chest tightened. Sylvia had a feeling she knew where this was going. "So Jake isn't safe here."

He shook his head. "No, he isn't. He's already been flown back to America."

For a second, the room tilted. She whispered, "No."

Finn leaned forward. "I'm sorry, Sylvia, but it's true. There was nothing I could do. I tried to suggest maybe you could mate him, but the DDA still said no. If an American visiting—or even joining—a dragon clan was murdered, it would cause major problems between the American and UK Department of Dragon Affairs branches. The US and UK governments didn't want to risk it."

She could feel the room closing in on her, but she fought against the oncoming panic and despair. She wouldn't let it win. Not this time. "Where is he? Back in San Francisco?"

"ADDA wouldn't say. All I know is that he's somewhere safe, near some Yank dragons who will watch out for him. And he'll stay there until the ADDA and DDA can ensure the threats are gone."

If he was near or staying with a dragon clan, then there was a chance Sylvia could see him. Maybe. Although it would take a giant leap of faith on her part.

And yet the thought of merely going back to her life without Jake—without his teasing or smiles or gentle protectiveness, or even how he looked at Sophie with love—seemed unbearable.

If Sylvia wanted a chance with him, she'd have to be bolder than she had been most of her life. Much like when she'd been in Glasgow last year and had dared to flirt with a stranger.

Before meeting Jake, she might've doubted that she could do it. But he'd shown her parts of herself she'd long hidden or had been afraid to embrace. Now was the time to be the female who went after what she wanted for once.

Her dragon murmured, *I know you're strong enough.*

Taking a deep breath, she blurted, "What if Sophie and I went to him? Do you think you could arrange that?"

Finn studied her for a second. "Cat's due any time now. Could you really leave her?"

No, she couldn't leave her eldest daughter and risk her dying in childbirth with Sylvia away.

However, after Cat gave birth, her daughter would most likely understand if she went away for a short while. Cat had her mate, and all of Sylvia's older children were adults.

Oh, aye, she'd miss spending more time with her first grandchild, but Sylvia wanted more than to be merely a mother or grandmother.

She also wanted to have a male like Jake in her life. Even if only for Sophie, she had to fight for him now or risk losing the closeness they'd gained over the last few days.

Maybe even lose him forever, if he was moved somewhere she couldn't go. For all she knew, Jake could be put into some sort of protective custody, far away from any dragon clans.

And Sylvia didn't want to miss the chance of better knowing the male she was already halfway in love with.

She replied, "I'll stay until after Cat gives birth and ensure she's fine. That should give me enough time to get things sorted. But after that, I want to take Sophie to be with Jake. Can you make that happen?"

Finn continued to watch her closely, his pupils flashing a few times between slits and round. "If I do, it'll involve a plane, and you know what that means."

Her dragon spoke up. *I understand. I don't mind you silencing me for a few days if it means we can see him again.*

Any dragon-shifter who wished to fly via airplane had to be injected with the dragon silent drug, which put their inner dragon into a sort of coma so they couldn't shift in midair and cause a disaster. *Are you sure? We've never had the shot before, and whilst rare, sometimes it has strange side effects.*

Her beast sniffed. *Of course I'm sure. Besides, we'll get to meet an American dragon clan. It would be fun to see how they do things. Maybe they have a few flying tricks I can learn.*

Sylvia nearly smiled at her dragon's words. *We'll see, dear heart, we'll see.*

She finally nodded at Finn. "I understand what it means. And a shot of the dragon silent drug is a small price to pay."

At least her daughter wouldn't have to get one since she was too young to shift.

He tapped his fingers against his desk. "Aye, then I'll try my hardest to make it happen. However I'd rather you take someone else with you, a familiar face to watch your back. Maybe one of your children?"

She had a feeling she'd ask Ian since he was the least likely to get into trouble abroad. "First see if I can go and then I'll decide on that."

Finn paused and finally asked, "Is this what you really want, Sylvia?"

She bobbed her head. "I...care for him, Finn. And he's Sophie's father. I want at least a chance to spend more time with Jake. It might not end up being forever, but I can't let him simply disappear without seeing how things turn out."

He stood. "Right, then I'll call in whatever favor I can. If you do go, I'll ask a favor of you, though. You'll most likely end up staying with a dragon clan. And if so, then maybe see if the leader is open to talking with me? It'd be good to have an ally in America."

Sylvia knew little of inter-clan politics, but she'd do anything for Finn. "I'll try."

He smiled at her. "Good. One way or another, I'll let you know as soon as possible about what they say."

After murmuring her gratitude and goodbye, Sylvia headed back to her cottage.

A few months ago, she'd never have imagined wanting to fly across an ocean to see someone.

And yet, she was more excited than anxious. Jake had come to Scotland for her. Now it was her turn to go to America for him.

Or at least she hoped she could. If only she knew how to reach Jake's cousin, the one who worked with the American Department of Dragon Affairs. Maybe she could help with Sylvia's case.

Then an idea hit her—she could ask Ian and Emma to use their computer skills to find out who she was. Maybe they could do that without doing anything illegal.

Surely having requests put in through both ends would help. Well, aye, provided his cousin would want to help.

But the more cards she held, the greater the chance she could win this odd little game.

And so she went to find her twin children to ask for a favor.

Chapter Seventeen

After nearly four weeks living with his cousin's dragon clan—PineRock—situated not far from Lake Tahoe on the California side, all Jake wanted to do was sneak off and hop on the first flight back to Scotland.

Not because the PineRock dragons and humans didn't welcome him or that his cousin and her dragon mate weren't going above and beyond by keeping him safe. No, it was because he wanted to talk with Sylvia and he wasn't allowed to make any sort of outside contact until ADDA said he could.

Some bullshit about safety or something.

He couldn't even send Sylvia a letter, as old-fashioned as that was these days.

For all intents and purposes, he'd just vanished, abandoning both Sylvia and Sophie without a word.

Sophie. He wondered for the thousandth time what other milestone he might've missed by now.

Or all the ones he'd miss in the future. Ones he and Sylvia should be cooing about together during the day.

And then sharing other joys at night.

He was about to do one of the things he despised the most—go down the road of what-ifs—when he heard his cousin Ashley's voice from behind him. "Glowering at trees again? Or maybe at the birds this time?"

He turned around and frowned at his dark-haired, fair-skinned cousin. The mischief dancing in her blue eyes didn't bode well. "What do you want?"

"And to think I told everyone how charming you were when you first arrived."

He sighed. "Sorry, Ash. I'm…not in a good mood. Being caged and useless, not to mention unable to see my daughter, is close to a nightmare for me."

"I know." Her expression softened as she took a step closer and touched his arm. "But I have news that might help."

Hope flickered in his chest. "They're letting me go free again?"

She shook her head, her long hair swaying in front of her. "No. Although I think this might be a very close second to freedom."

He narrowed his eyes and growled, "Just tell me already, Ashley. I'm not in the mood for games."

She shrugged one shoulder. "I'm mated to a dragon-shifter, Jake. Growling doesn't work on me." Just as he was about to do it again, she put up a hand. "But I promised Wes I wouldn't give away the surprise. So stop growling and just follow me."

And without waiting for him to reply, she strode off, and Jake had to quicken his pace to keep up with her. "Is it something to do with Ben?"

Ben was Ashley and Wes's young son. And while they were in no way conscious of causing him pain, being around his cousin's child only made him miss Sophie even more.

"No. Ben is with his grandma Cynthia for a few hours." She glanced over at him. "And keep asking questions if you want, but you know how well I can keep a secret."

"What, like how you kept your burning lust for Wes hidden for years until the two of you finally came to your senses?"

Ashley's cheeks tinged pink. "Can we not talk about my lust? You're my cousin, and it's weird."

He smiled, which was rare for Jake these days. "I think every single clan member I've met has told me your and Wes's story. It's kind of hard not to bring it up."

She narrowed her eyes at him. "Maybe, but *you* don't have to bring it up every day."

He full-on grinned. "But it's fun. I'm bored and need something to do, after all."

And teasing Ashley helped him forget about who he'd rather be teasing and laughing with.

Before he could think yet again of Sylvia and Sophie, Ashley's reply garnered his attention. "Well, being bored might not be a problem for much longer." She stopped walking and he did as well. "How about we race back to my place? It's been a while since I've beaten you. Unless you're too old now?"

He quirked an eyebrow. "That was more than twenty years ago, *and* you cheated."

She raised her head a fraction. "I never cheated. I merely scoped out the racecourse ahead of time and knew which shortcuts to take."

He rolled his eyes. "That's still cheating."

She waved a hand in dismissal. "This isn't a camping trip to Yosemite. We both know the way between here and my home. And I promise not to take any shortcuts, only the direct path. Ready?"

He raised an eyebrow. "Are you sure you're a mother and a dragon clan leader's wife?"

She grinned. "Of course. But having a little fun isn't something you should forget as you get older. Besides, your surprise is waiting at the end of it."

He sighed. "Fine. All of my bruises have healed up, so it should be fair."

"Good." Ashley readied herself. "On the count of three. One, two, three!"

As she raced off, Jake followed. His cousin was faster, but he was slightly taller, and he soon caught up to her.

They had just about reached her home when he noticed someone sitting in front of the window to the living room, and he stopped in his tracks.

Could it be? He walked a little closer until he made out Sylvia's dark hair, small nose, and full lips. Her eyes were closed as she tilted her face into the sunshine.

He blinked, but she didn't disappear.

Somehow, someway, Sylvia was here. On PineRock.

Jake raced into the house and hoped like hell he wasn't imagining things.

SYLVIA TRIED her best to smile at the pale, ginger-haired American dragon leader named Wes Dalton, but she couldn't quite manage it.

Not only was her dragon still silent because of the drug she'd had to take in order to fly, but the number of flight transfers and then a long car drive to get to Clan PineRock—the American dragon clan nestled some miles away from the nearest human city—had sapped most of her energy. Add in taking care of her daughter over all those miles, and Sylvia could barely keep her eyes open.

Maybe under other circumstances she'd enjoy the massive pine forests that put most in the UK to shame, or the hills and peaks that were similar yet different from Scotland, or even wish to see more of the beautiful, blue Lake Tahoe she'd glimpsed on her way here from the Las Vegas airport.

However, for the moment, she merely held Sophie close and allowed her son Jamie to chat away with Wes while Sylvia tried to stay awake.

She'd wanted to bring Ian, but Jamie had begged to come to America. And sensing her youngest son needed a chance to be someplace where he wasn't merely one of the MacAllister brood—one where he had been the youngest for more than twenty years— she'd given in. He had a way with Sophie, too, which had come in handy on the various flights.

But her son loved to talk, and of course that meant poor Wes had to endure his chatter. Jamie had now moved from learning about the dragon clans in the area to asking about any football teams nearby. Once Wes established he meant soccer and not American football, they'd started discussing how they should start a team or two in the area.

As she studied the American dragon leader, she had to admit he seemed genuinely interested in what Jamie had to say. Male bonding, she supposed.

Hmm, maybe Jamie could get to know Wes better

and then ask him to reach out to Finn. That could work.

She'd ask him to do it later. For now, however, Sylvia merely sat on the chair near the window and held her daughter close. And as the sun warmed her, she soon half dozed until she heard the front door bang open, and seconds later, Jake stood in the doorway.

His ginger hair was windswept, his hazel eyes bright, and his cheeks slightly flushed above his close-cut beard. He was gorgeous, as always, and all she could think of was how much she wanted to kiss him again.

If he still wanted to kiss her, that was. Sylvia still didn't know how he'd taken Arlo's kidnapping. One of her fears was that Jake blamed Sylvia for it.

The conversation died in the room as Jake walked toward her. Sylvia slowly stood to avoid waking her daughter, her heart thudding in her chest. She watched his eyes, looking for anger, or disdain, or any other number of negative emotions.

But all she saw was joy and relief.

Maybe he didn't blame her after all.

Jake gently cupped her cheek. "Are you really here?"

Leaning into his touch, she inhaled the mixture of pine and spicy male, her worry fading as some of her tiredness melted away. "Aye, I am."

He pressed a gentle kiss to her lips, erasing even

more of her built-up tension, before doing the same to Sophie's forehead. "Hello, little one." He brushed Sophie's hair from her forehead as their daughter stirred a wee it. "Daddy's missed you." Emotion choked Sylvia's throat as Jake looked back into her eyes. "And you."

Her voice cracked as she began, "Jake—"

Wes's voice interrupted her. "We'll just leave you two alone for a little while. Come on, Jamie. I'll show you where you'll be staying and then introduce you to some of the other young males here."

Sylvia barely noticed the others leave. But once the door clicked close, she cleared her throat and tried again. "I hope it's okay I came. I just needed to see you again and knew this was the only way I could do it."

Jake brushed her cheek with the back of his fingers. "Of course it's fine you came. I wanted to go back to you, but they wouldn't let me."

A whisper of guilt raced through her. "That's partially my fault. I'm sure they've told you about Arlo and why he took you."

He growled, "The jealous bastard and his actions aren't your fault, Sylvia. Don't ever think that."

She searched his gaze. "But if not for me, you wouldn't be banished here, unable to see your family and run your restaurants."

He stroked his thumb against her cheek. "It's not exactly banishment, my dragon lady. And now that you're here, staying with PineRock just got a whole hell of a lot better."

She tried searching his eyes to see if he was merely trying to make her feel better. But all she saw was happiness and something she couldn't define in his gaze.

Did he truly not blame her at all for his circumstances?

At this point, her dragon would usually speak up. But she couldn't, and Sylvia sighed at the silence.

He murmured, "What's wrong?"

She shook her head. "It's silly. I'm just tired is all."

He rubbed her upper arm. "Tell me."

"Well, in order to fly, I had to silence my dragon for a few days. And it's a wee bit…strange. I know you've never had to worry about another voice in your head, but it's like half of me is missing."

He gently took Sophie from her, held the baby in one arm, and then pulled her close to his side with the other. She melted against him without a thought as he asked, "She'll come back, though, right?"

"Aye, she should. Very rarely the dragon stays silent longer, sometimes forever, but it's unlikely."

He squeezed her gently, and Sylvia took strength from the gesture. He replied, "Well, is there anything we can do to help bring her back sooner? I rather miss asking you what she's saying."

She smiled up at him. "You just want her to say some more dirty words, aye?"

He winked. "Of course." He nuzzled her cheek a second before adding, "But if there's anything I can do, tell me." He paused a second before asking, "Unless you have to fly right back?"

She shook her head. "Your cousin Ashley is quite a marvel, really. Between her and a few humans both on Stonefire and Lochguard, they managed to get me an extended stay. Something about a trial run for better relations between the UK and America. Although I do have to write an official report at the end of my time here, but that was hardly a reason to keep me from coming."

He smiled at her. "So not only did our one-night stand give us dear Sophie, it might change US and UK relations for the better."

Sylvia snorted. "That's a bit much." And the devil in her, the one that loved to tease when around Jake, came out. "I assure you, your cock isn't *that* important."

Jake laughed, and the sound washed away much of her exhaustion and anxiety. She'd worried about things being awkward, or it being a mistake to come halfway around the world just to see him. But his laughter made it all worth it.

Of course it was loud and unplanned, so Sophie scrunched her wee nose and finally opened her eyes. Before she could wail, Jake released Sylvia to bring Sophie up to his chest, to his eye level. He bopped her nose as he also made funny faces at her.

And then Sophie laughed for the very first time and Sylvia stopped breathing.

Jake noticed it and murmured, "What is it?"

"She hasn't laughed before." She met his gaze. "That was the first time."

Pride filled his eyes before he looked back at their daughter. "Well, now your daddy has three gifts all in one day. You, your mom, and now your first laugh." He kissed Sophie's cheek and Sylvia's heart melted. "Now I'll have to see just how many times I can get you to laugh to make your mom happy."

Tears threatened to fall, but Sylvia took a deep breath and kept them back. She was absolutely *not* going to cry today.

No, she wanted to spend time with Jake and try to enjoy it while she still could.

Because even though she hadn't told him yet, she knew that if they did decide they wanted to mate, it would mean not only him giving up his life back in San Francisco for good, but Sylvia would most likely have to give up hers back in Scotland too.

Until the DDA and ADDA declared it safe for Jake, he couldn't go back to the UK.

So if he did eventually want to mate her—and she was hoping more and more he would—she would probably have to live in America for a while.

Which meant not seeing her older children every day like she was used to.

But all of that was a big what-if. She would take

each day as it came, ensure Jake got to spend as much time with Sophie as possible, and go from there.

And not for the first time, she wished her dragon was back to tell her it would be all right in the end.

Chapter Eighteen

E ven with Sophie's slight weight in his arm and Sylvia standing next to him, Jake still couldn't believe his two ladies were here.

He raised a hand to touch Sylvia's face again, running his thumb over her bottom lip, loving how her breath hitched at the touch.

He loved his daughter and was beyond thrilled she was here, but he desperately needed to claim Sylvia. And soon.

Not just because his cock wanted it, either. No, he needed to reassure her in every way possible that he didn't blame her for Arlo's fuckery, how he burned for her and wanted to reward her bravery in risking it all to come see him.

Especially coming to the US meant Sylvia giving up so much for him—spending time with her other children, silencing her dragon, and being surrounded by the familiar instead of a clan full of strangers.

First things first—he wanted to erase any doubts Sylvia had about him still wanting her. Leaning over, he nipped her earlobe before murmuring, "I want to hear everything that's happened since I last saw you, I promise." He moved his head until his lips were nearly touching hers. "But I need you, Sylvia. As soon as possible. To ensure you're real, and I'm not dreaming that my kind, brave, pretty dragon lady is really here with me."

She smiled up at him, the sight making his heart pound harder—damn, he'd missed her—and she placed a hand on his chest. "I'm here, I assure you." She stroked slowly, each pass sending blood straight to his cock, no matter how he fought it. "If you take me to where you're staying, then we can see to Sophie, probably get her to sleep rather easily given all the travel, and then say hello properly whilst naked."

He chuckled. "There's the lady I first met, the dragonwoman who couldn't wait to get into my pants."

She rolled her eyes. "I can wait. You're the one who said you needed me, remember?"

Moving his mouth to her ear again, he worried her earlobe with his teeth before whispering, "If I didn't have a baby in my arms, it'd be easy to make you beg for more, my dragon lady. I'll just have to show you soon enough."

He moved his mouth to her neck, and could feel the rapid beat of her pulse. Kissing her there, she arched her head back. "We need to stop, Jake. I'm not going to let you take me in the clan leader's living room."

He nibbled her neck lightly before raising his head, grinning at her. "I'm sure sex on their couch isn't exactly the best way to make a good impression."

She snorted. "Aye, it's not." She moved her hand to his bicep and squeezed. "I'm a sure thing, Jake Swift, so let's get settled and then we'll see if you can live up to all these promises of yours."

Sophie decided at that moment to start babbling, as if to distract her parents from kissing, and more, in front of her.

Jake moved back, readjusted his grip on Sophie, and said to his daughter, "Don't worry, little one. We'll wait until you're asleep. And Mommy and Daddy are going to spoil you rotten until you do finally take a nap."

His daughter lightly hit him on the chest with her palm before grabbing his shirt into a baby death grip and pulling.

Jake laughed. "Missed your dad, huh?"

Sylvia said softly, "She has. Terribly. Even though she can't talk, I could tell."

He looked back at his dragonwoman. "I hated leaving you to take care of her alone again."

Sylvia took Sophie's free hand between her fingers. "It wasn't so bad. She cried a lot at first, but what with Cat giving birth and the whirlwind packing for this trip, she must've sensed something was going on and was on her best behavior."

"Cat gave birth?"

Sylvia nodded. "A daughter they named Felicity. Later, I can show you more photos than you'll ever want to see of her."

He reached up his hand to caress her cheek. "You gave up time with your first grandchild to see me."

She placed her hand over his. "Felicity arrived two weeks ago, so I spent as much time with her as I could whilst I waited for all the paperwork to go through. But as much as a piece of my heart stayed behind with her, I couldn't just abandon you. Not for Sophie's sake. Cat understood that and encouraged me to come here."

He searched her eyes. "And what about you? Did you come for your sake too?"

She hesitated a second, and he wished it didn't make his heart hurt. She finally said, "Aye, well, that is a very serious conversation. And one I'm not about to have when I'm in desperate need of food, a shower, and some sleep." He opened his mouth, but she beat him to it. "Just know that I've missed you too, Jake. Crazy as it sounds, given how little time we've spent together, the house seemed empty with you gone."

He more than understood, as his own place on PineRock had been too damned quiet without her and Sophie. Hell, he'd even missed her noisy, overprotective children.

However, at Sylvia voicing her needs, he saw the circles under her eyes and the way she leaned against him for support.

His dragon lady was tired and barely standing.

And suddenly he felt like an ass for wanting to get her naked and under him so quickly.

So he put an arm around her shoulders and guided her toward the hall that would lead to the doorway. "Come on. You'll be staying with me, and my house isn't far from here. I'll ensure you're taken care of, tie you to the bed if need be to make you sleep, and make sure you and Sophie are settled before anything else."

Sylvia leaned her head on his shoulder. "Maybe if I were twenty years younger, I could power on through another day without sleep, but I'm not. And Sophie doesn't like flying much, so let's just say some peace and quiet will be heaven." She looked up again. "Although I hope you'll sleep with me again."

A sudden need to hold her for as long as she needed coursed through him. "You'd be hard-pressed to stop me."

Wrapping her arm around his back and toward

his waist, she put her head back on his shoulder as they walked. "Good. With my dragon silent, it's harder to fall asleep since I haven't truly been alone since I was six years old—that's when my dragon first spoke with me." She squeezed her arm around him. "However, with you next to me, I won't be alone anymore."

He couldn't help but feel guilty at how Sylvia had willingly silenced such an essential part of herself— her inner dragon—just to come see him.

Jake would never be able to make up for that, but he would spend every moment trying his damnedest to do so. "Then how about this? We'll get Sophie settled, and then I'll merely hold you while you sleep. We can have all the discussions and such you want later."

She smiled up at him. "That sounds perfect."

And at the pure happiness shining in her eyes, Jake fell a little in love with her. He'd been going crazy being trapped on PineRock, when all he'd wanted to do was help take care of Sophie and Sylvia.

He'd thought maybe it was just a whirlwind of finding out he had a daughter, blistering sex with Sylvia, and the newness of living with dragon-shifters that made him want to be so easily at her side.

However, it was her. She needed him in a way no one else did, and he took pleasure in being the one to help take care of her, help coax out her playfulness and be the one to show her that it was okay to have a second chance at life.

Jake had a feeling that for too long Sylvia had hidden herself from the world to focus solely on her children. Almost as if it was the only way to guard her heart against the loss of her mate, the pressures of her in-laws, and the feeling she'd failed her kids.

But there was so much more to her. And Jake hoped he could spend more time, maybe even forever, getting to unpack and know every little bit she kept tucked away.

As they exited Wes and Ashley's house, he put those thoughts aside for now. First things first—he had to take care of his two travel-weary dragon ladies.

The more serious conversation awaiting him and Sylvia would come soon enough.

But until then, he cradled Sophie against him and squeezed his arm around Sylvia's waist, reminding him how he wasn't in a dream and that they really were with him in the flesh again.

And if he had any say in it, he hoped they always would be.

Chapter Nineteen

Connor MacAllister approached Aimee King's cottage and took a second to go through his options.

With all the hubbub of his sister Cat giving birth and his mum going to America, he hadn't had a lot of free time.

As a result, it meant he hadn't been able to walk past Aimee's cottage like he normally did, not for a couple weeks now.

Aye, he'd thought of sending her a note, but he didn't want to scare her. After all, it'd taken months for the female to gather enough courage to merely open her window and wave at him.

But maybe now she thought he'd forgotten her or didn't care, or maybe even had retreated once more after some sort of setback.

Which meant she might not come to the window again, maybe never.

And for some reason, he didn't like that.

His dragon sighed. *Don't just stand here. That won't accomplish anything.*

It's a delicate situation, dragon. As you well know.

His beast sighed. *Aye, but she's come a long way from arriving on Lochguard. And knocking on a door isn't going to send her into a fit.*

You don't know that.

Maybe not. But I do know that if she can't learn to come out of that house more than once every few weeks, she'll never be able to enjoy life again.

While Connor didn't know all the details of what had happened before coming to Lochguard, he knew Aimee had been tossed into prison by the old Skyhunter leader at age eighteen and had stayed there for five long years. Everyone assumed Aimee had been tortured in some manner, given how her dragon was silent. That only happened because of drugs, severe trauma, or a combination of the two.

Or so he'd read. Connor had secretly been learning more and more about inner dragons over the last few months. He wasn't a doctor, but for some reason, he wanted to know more about Aimee and what was or wasn't possible for her now.

He may not be able to help her talk to her beast again or even encourage her to shift if her dragon did return, but he could distract her, make her smile, and maybe teach her to trust him a wee bit. Not all males were bad, and if he could be the one to remind her of that, then he'd be content.

Mostly.

However, no matter how bonny she was, Connor wasn't going to imagine more.

Aye, well, not in reality. He couldn't contain his dreams of the lass smiling and welcoming him. Teasing him freely and not holding back.

Being the female she could've been had she lived a normal life.

But she hadn't had a normal life, and Connor knew it. So pushing aside those thoughts, he readjusted the container in his hands. Cat had mentioned once how Aimee liked biscuits, so he'd made some chocolate chip ones for her.

Right, then. He'd put it off long enough. So Connor stepped onto the path, looked up at her window, and waited to see if she'd show.

One minute passed, and then another. Even after five minutes, she didn't appear.

He had one last option before the door-knocking. So he picked up a wee pebble and tossed it against the window. And then again with another.

No dark-haired lass came to the window.

Connor was just debating whether he should knock when Aimee's slight form appeared in the window.

As she scanned the path and spotted him, he

waved. And for a second, Aimee merely stood there, her face expressionless.

Then she opened the window. "What?"

Connor resisted frowning at the irritation in her voice. He'd never heard that before. Aye, they hadn't talked much, but she'd always been shy and kind before.

He lifted the biscuits. "I'm going to leave these biscuits here for you."

"Why?"

At her curt tone, he wondered if she were angry at him. "As an apology. I didn't mean to miss our near-daily greetings, but a lot has happened to my family lately." He paused and then blurted, "I was going to send a message but didn't know if you'd want it."

Her posture relaxed a fraction. Her voice was soft as she answered, "I had hoped you would say something about why you haven't been around." Her next words were merely a whisper, but he heard it easily thanks to his supersensitive hearing. "No one tells me anything, after all. And I…well…going out is difficult for me."

It was the first time she'd ever been so honest with him and said more than a few words about the weather or asked what he was going to cook that day.

Ignoring the small thrill that shot through him, he cleared his throat and smiled up at her. Deciding to push her a wee bit, he asked, "So are we friends then?"

She looked off to the side and lightly traced the edge of the window frame. "I had hoped we were."

Oh, lass. He hated that she had to doubt it.

He nodded enthusiastically. "Of course we're friends." He placed the container on her front stoop and then raced back enough to see her again. "Give me a request, Aimee. And I'll do whatever you want."

She smiled shyly as her green eyes met his again. "I like it when you surprise me."

Even though his dragon kept silent around Aimee since flashing dragon eyes still frightened her, Connor could sense his dragon's approval.

And so he backed up, ran, and managed a series of flips until he was on the other side in front of her cottage.

As he stuck his landing, he grinned up at her and she clapped. "That was brilliant."

At the happiness in her eyes, Connor decided talking with her via window wasn't nearly enough.

Aye, it'd take time and patience, but he was determined to sit across from Aimee King, talk with her, and be the friend she desperately needed.

The hard part would be not wanting more from her.

Chapter Twenty

Sylvia awoke to strong arms wrapped around her and a rather noticeable hardness against her arse.

She didn't have to open her eyes to know it was Jake. She'd recognize his heat and his scent anywhere.

Just as she contemplated teasing him awake, his hot breath blew against her ear as he said, "Good morning."

Opening her eyes, she saw light filtering through the curtains. "What? It's the next day?"

Nuzzling her neck, he said, "Yes. Don't you remember? You fed Sophie a few times, although you were barely awake. Maybe you can do it asleep now?"

She lightly ran her finger across the hairs of his forearm. "Aye, I don't have to be fully awake. It's just routine—feed and fall back asleep. But I still can't imagine sleeping for that long."

Jake kissed her neck, sending a shiver through her body, before replying, "It's okay to sleep if you need it. You were tired, Sylvia." A hand moved up to her breast to tweak her sensitive nipple—grateful dragon-shifters didn't leak like many humans—and she bit back a groan as he continued, "Although I hope you're rested now."

Wiggling her arse against his erection, she smiled at his moan. "Aye, I am. So I can go make the rounds of meeting people. Maybe visit with the schoolchildren to talk about Lochguard, better get to know your cousin. See how PineRock is different from Lochguard. I should get up and start it all."

He nipped where her neck met her shoulder. "You can do that later."

Reaching back, she dug her fingers into his arse cheek. "Why? Did you have other plans?"

He kissed his way up her neck until he could nibble her earlobe, and Sylvia melted a little more against him. "I thought my mouth could get to know your body again. You know, just to make sure I haven't forgotten a single curve or valley."

She snorted. "You're going to have to work on those lines, aye?"

The hand that had been playing with her nipples slowly moved down her belly and stopped just short of between her thighs. "Considering you said you're a sure thing, maybe I should use the cheesiest ones I can think of."

She couldn't stop smiling. "Such as?"

His finger stroked through her pussy once, and Sylvia bit her lip to keep from begging for more. At least not yet. She liked teasing Jake, missed it, and wanted a bit of fun before riding him.

He murmured into her ear, "How about this one: you and I are like nachos with jalapeños. I'm cheesy, you're super hot, and we belong together."

She rolled her eyes. "Aye, that is fairly awful."

He stroked between her thighs again, and it took most of her willpower to concentrate on his words instead of the way his thumb slowly circled her clit. "I have one more that suits us well since we both run restaurants. Do you know what's on the menu?"

He increased the pressure against her, and Sylvia barely managed to get out, "What?"

"Me. N. U."

She laughed. "That's even worse."

He removed his hand, and she almost drew it back. However, Jake moved them so she was on her back and he was above her. He stroked the corner of her mouth with his thumb. With his hot body pressed against hers, she nearly started purring. Jake spoke before she could, though. "I think I'm going to have to find some more cheesy pick-up lines so that I can make you laugh every morning and night with a new one."

And there he went being kind and romantic again, making her heart swell.

Aye, a female could get used to waking up to him every day.

Sylvia reached up to stroke his cheek. "You're such a good male, Jake. I still can't believe you're real."

Removing his hand, he lowered his face closer to hers until his breath danced against her lips as he replied, "I can think of one way to show how very real I am." He rubbed his cock against her slit. "What do you say? I'm more than up for it, as you can tell."

He winked, and she giggled. "Are you sure you're in your forties and not a teenager?"

"I only act like a horny teenager around you, Sylvia."

He moved his hips against her again and she clutched his shoulders, digging in her nails. "Then let's hope you don't completely act like a teenager because if you come after a minute or two, I may have to rethink staying here."

With a growl, he took her lips in a rough kiss, nipping, licking, and stroking, until Sylvia was all but grinding against his cock, wanting more than his kisses.

When Jake finally pulled away, she itched to bring his head back. However, he spoke before she could. "Trust me, I want to be deep inside you right now, but I need a condom, love. Which means I have to get up."

Sylvia didn't release her hold on him. Even though she had no right to say it, she blurted, "You don't have to." He raised his brows and she continued, "It's unlikely to happen since I'm still breastfeeding Sophie. But if it did, I wouldn't mind one more bairn, provided you're there with me."

As he studied her, Sylvia did her best to contain her emotions. It was a cowardly way to see how he felt, and she knew it. If her dragon were around, she probably would've stopped her.

But her beast remained silent, and so Sylvia would have to face this herself for once.

And the last thing she wanted to do was truly pressure him. So she opened her mouth to say she'd been stupid when he took her lips in another searing kiss. When he finally let her up for air, he murmured, "I would love nothing more than to have another child, but I think we should wait. Too much remains unsettled."

Before she could say another word, he kissed her again, stroked between her thighs with his fingers, and made her forget about anything but him.

Soon he released her lips and kissed down her body, taking time to lick one nipple and then the other, before kissing her belly and then spreading her thighs wide.

Anticipation built as he stared at her, making her

hotter and wetter. She squirmed. She was just about to reach for his head and push him where she wanted him when a loud doorbell rang through the house.

Jake growled, "Ignore it," before he kissed her pussy, licked it, and tortured her clit with his teeth and tongue.

However, he'd barely gotten started when it rang again, and again, and again in rapid succession, as if someone was hitting it over and over again on purpose.

A beat later, Sophie's cry filled the air too.

With a growl, Jake rolled off the bed. "It'd better be a fucking emergency or I'm going to have more than a few words to say."

"I'm sure it's important." Sylvia jumped out of bed. "I'll handle Sophie and you go see who's at the door."

With a nod, Jake went down the stairs and Sylvia went to their daughter, hoping it wasn't anything too urgent. After all, they'd have more than enough drama for a lifetime. Sylvia would gladly welcome a wee bit of boring.

JAKE STOMPED TO THE DOOR, peeked through the eyehole, and wrenched it open with a growl, revealing PineRock's head Protector, Cristina Juarez. "What?"

She merely raised a dark eyebrow. "Just save your breath, Jake. I wouldn't be here if it wasn't important. It's about your sister."

His anger faded. "What happened?"

She looked pointedly over his shoulder. "I'd rather not discuss it out in the open."

He stepped back and Cris walked past him into the living room.

The tall, light-brown-skinned female pinned him with her brown eyes and didn't waste time on niceties. "She showed up this morning without any sort of papers. Even asked directions along the way, alerting who the hell knows how many people of her destination. If ADDA find her here, she could be in a lot of trouble. And before you say send her away, I tried. Even without us saying a word, she's convinced you're here and wants to talk with you."

Jake had a feeling he knew which sister, but he still asked, "Did she give her name?"

"No, but Ashley recognized her. It's Lila."

He sighed. Lila had always been the most protective of him. Apparently the brief note the US and UK dragon departments had let him write to his family hadn't been enough to placate her. "Let me get dressed and I'll convince her to leave."

"Do it quickly. The longer she's on PineRock's lands, the greater chance she's in danger. Not just from ADDA, either. The AHOL fuckers have been hiding out in the forests more and more lately."

AHOL was the acronym of a group called America for Humans Only League, who were hell-bent on ridding the US of anything dragon-shifter. Most people called them the League, but he had to admit AHOL was more fitting since they were indeed a bunch of assholes.

Jake nodded. "It won't take long."

Just as he turned away, Cris added, "And bring Sylvia and Sophie. She might not know they're here, but if she sees you're not alone, it might more easily convince her to leave."

He doubted it. If anything, it'd convince Lila to stay longer. "I'll ask Sylvia. Now, go. Time is of the essence, as you said."

Racing up the stairs, he reached the top quickly and went into the room used for Sophie. Sylvia must've finished feeding their daughter because Sophie now wore an adorable outfit with a baby dragon playing in a field of flowers on the front.

The second Sylvia met his gaze, her smiled faded and she frowned. "What's wrong?"

"My sister Lila showed up here without permission, and she refuses to leave until she sees me." He quickly explained how she could get in trouble from not only ADDA, but could be hurt by the League members too before adding, "I need to see her. It's up to you if you want to come with me."

"Do you want me to come?" she asked gingerly.

If his sister wasn't breaking the law, he would've

immediately screamed yes. Instead, he wanted to be cautious, so he replied, "You coming might make her even more stubborn in refusing to leave."

"If you don't want me to meet her, just say so, Jake."

He mentally cursed, crossed the room, and cupped her cheek. "Of course I want her to meet you. I'm just afraid it'll make Lila dig in her heels about not wanting to leave. Meeting her niece for a few minutes won't be enough. I just know it."

She searched his gaze. "Is there a way for her to stay here too? Given what you told me about her grief for her son, it could be a nice change of pace. She could also get to know Sophie."

He resisted a frown. "Lila's never shown an interest in dragon-shifters before."

"Aye, well, I never showed an interest in human males before you. Sometimes life takes unexpected turns and results in changes we never saw coming."

He took her face in his hands. "That's true. I didn't see you coming."

She placed a hand over one of his. "From what I can tell, you've been protecting your sister since your nephew's death. Maybe just ask her what she wants. If someone had done that for me instead of assuming what was best, maybe I would've realized there was more to me than being a mum long before I was ill." She stroked the back of his hand with her thumb. "Grief for a loved one never truly goes away. But finding a small reason to try for more, to finally be brave enough to no longer use grief as a shield, aye, well, that's everything. I'd hate for your sister to suffer as long as I did when you might be able to help her now."

His first instinct was to keep his sister as safe as possible, back home near her children and other family.

And yet, that would be assuming or deciding something that Lila should do for herself. And Jake wasn't going to be like all the dragons back on Lochguard who'd thought they knew what was best for Sylvia, all while never taking into consideration her wants or needs.

He leaned in and gently kissed Sylvia. "You're so wise."

She smiled. "I have my moments, aye."

He grinned and then kissed her again before replying, "Then give me Sophie and get dressed so we can all go meet with Lila."

She handed over their daughter. "Just give me a few minutes."

As they both quickly dressed and left the house, Jake carried his daughter close and held Sylvia's hand with his free one. While he wished his sister would've waited, at least Sylvia and Sophie would finally get to meet one of his siblings.

And who knew—maybe Lila would end up

staying on PineRock and maybe even smile again, like she had before tragedy had struck her.

Either way, it would be her decision. And he had Sylvia to thank for letting him realize how important that was.

Jake squeezed her hand and she glanced over at him. He merely shook his head, brought her hand up to kiss it, and then murmured, "I'm glad you're here."

When she beamed at him, his heart skipped a beat. Somehow, someway, he'd discover how to win her over completely.

But first, he needed to deal with his sister.

SYLVIA'S HEART thudded in her chest as they entered the building used by PineRock's Protectors. She shouldn't worry so much about meeting Jake's sister, and yet she couldn't help it.

Meeting family was usually a big step, although she and Jake had never done things in order when it came to relationships. So she really shouldn't put too much importance or meaning on it.

No doubt her dragon would say the same.

Bloody hell, being without her dragon for the first time in decades was harder than she'd ever imagined. Sylvia missed her more than anything.

However, coming after Jake had been the right choice. She just knew it.

Besides, her dragon should return in a day or two. Fingers crossed.

Jake squeezed her hand in his and she met his smiling gaze. He murmured, "Don't worry. Be yourself and you'll do fine."

She nodded and he handed Sophie over to her as they reached a door guarded by a tall dragon-shifter, a female she vaguely recalled meeting the night before. But since she'd been so exhausted, she couldn't recall her name.

However, Jake did. "Tell me you aren't going in with us, Cris."

The dragonwoman shrugged a shoulder. "I'll stay out here and act as guard. As much as I want to trust you, I can't risk your sister fleeing on her own. She'll need an escort when she leaves, to protect against the League."

Sylvia had vaguely read about the anti-dragon group. They were a bit more militant and obsessive than the dragon hunters back in the UK. She didn't envy the American dragon-shifters dealing with that lot, not at all.

Jake replied, "I know. Although send for Ashley. And if possible, for Wes, too. We might need to talk to them afterward."

Cris merely nodded and Jake moved his gaze to Sylvia's. "Ready?"

She readjusted her hold on Sophie and nodded. "Aye, of course."

He kissed her quickly before opening the door and leading her inside.

A human female with auburn hair streaked with gray stood at the far side, her arms crossed over her chest and her brows drawn together in a frown. However, as soon as she saw Jake, the female's gaze turned softer. "I knew you had to be here, Jake."

He released his hold on Sylvia to hug his sister. "As good as it is to see you, you shouldn't have come, Lila."

The female raised a brow. "As if 'shouldn't' would stop me. I've been looking after you since you were fifteen, Jake, and I'm not about to stop anytime soon."

"Ever the big sister." Jake shook his head as he stepped back. He motioned toward Sylvia. "Lila, this is Sylvia and Sophie MacAllister, my girlfriend and daughter, respectively. Sylvia, this is my oldest sister, Lila Herrera."

Sylvia smiled and forced herself to walk over to Jake's sister. Although, as the human smiled at her, Sylvia's tension eased considerably. "Nice to meet you, Lila."

Lila replied, "You too. To be honest, I couldn't believe it when Jake told me he had a daughter, and yet I'm glad he does. The love and excitement every time he spoke of Sophie says volumes." Lila put out her arms. "Can I hold my niece?"

Sylvia didn't hesitate to do so. And Sophie merely

stared up at her aunt with her big eyes, and Sylvia waited to see how she'd react.

But then Lila tickled her chin and side and Sophie smiled.

Jake placed a hand on Sylvia's lower back before saying, "I think she has a thing for Americans. Maybe it's the accent."

Sylvia snorted. "Nothing to do with the person itself, aye? Just the accent. Maybe I should test out your theory."

Amusement danced in his eyes. "Going to go American for a little while then, my dragon lady?"

She tried her best to mimic his accent. "Maybe something like this? Do I sound American now?"

He chuckled and kissed her cheek. "Don't ever try that again. I much prefer your lyrical Scottish accent."

"Good because the flat vowels would be the death of me."

He laughed. "Can't have death by vowels, now, can we?"

As she lightly smacked his chest, Lila cleared her throat. Sylvia couldn't help but blush. After all, here she was teasing Jake and all but ignoring his sister. She looked at Lila. "Sorry. Something about your brother brings out the devil in me."

But as the human female smiled slowly, Sylvia's unease faded. Lila replied, "No need to apologize. Seeing my brother happy makes me happy." She paused a beat and then asked, "But be that as it may, how did you end up here in America? Did you come with Jake? The last time I talked with him, you both were in Scotland."

Sylvia sighed. "Aye, well, that's a long story and one I don't know if I'm at liberty to share."

Lila frowned and glanced at her brother. "First, you tell me that you can't say anything. And now Sylvia. Just what's going on, Jake?"

There was a knock on the door, and Ashley Swift walked into the room. "I'm back."

Lila stared at her cousin. "Can you talk now? Or are all of you going to look shifty and simply say over and over again that you can't tell me anything?"

Ashley sighed. "I no longer have a choice but to spill the beans."

Jake asked, "What do you mean?"

She gestured for them all to sit. Once they complied, Ashley answered, "Some of the Protectors found and tried to catch some League members lurking in the forest. However, they only caught one, and the others escaped." Ashley looked pointedly at Lila. "Which means they no doubt have your picture and will add it to their collection."

"Collection?" Sylvia echoed.

Ashley switched her gaze to Sylvia. "Yes. The League has started keeping a running tab of who visits dragon clans or interacts with dragon-shifters. Obviously they can't keep track of every single person, but they've made PineRock one of their prime targets, along with the other clans near here. And before you ask why, just know that some powerful humans in the area have made it happen. Partly it's my fault, but that's neither here nor there. The important thing is that they'll now keep track of Lila's comings and goings, at least for a while."

Lila shook her head. "But we don't have a big League problem in the Bay Area."

"Perhaps not, but from what my ADDA sources say, there's a secret online database. Your picture will be there."

Lila readjusted her hold on Sophie before saying, "It's not like I can hide out forever, though. Nor am I going to cower inside my house."

Ashley shook her head. "Of course not. But Jake had told me how, before the whole kidnapping business in Scotland, he'd planned a trip for you, Ada, and your families."

Lila narrowed her eyes. "What kidnapping business?"

Oh, dear. Certainly Ashley had let that slip on purpose? Sylvia couldn't imagine her doing so by accident.

Sylvia remained quiet, wanting to hear what Ashley suggested. Sylvia was, after all, a guest on PineRock and supposedly the first candidate for the UK-US dragon trial program. She couldn't risk saying something she shouldn't.

Thankfully Jake's cousin didn't hesitate. "That's why Jake's here, staying with me and Wes. A dragon-shifter kidnapped him, and they're trying to ensure no one else is out to get him back in Scotland."

Lila looked at her brother and then to Sylvia. "Which explains why you're here in the US, right, Sylvia? Because Jake needed to leave Scotland." She nodded, and Lila looked back at Ashley. "I'm going to ask for more details later, but for now—what does Jake's planned vacation have to do with anything?"

Ashley leaned forward. "Wes has been talking with Lochguard's clan leader, as well as with ADDA and the UK Department of Dragon Affairs. They're close to ferreting out the two others they think were helping the dragonman who kidnapped Jake. If—and it's still uncertain at this point—they can catch them, then it's probably in your best interest to go on the trip Jake planned. A few weeks away should help the League focus on others."

Sylvia, whose clan had been dealing with anti-dragon enemies for a while now, spoke up. "And if it doesn't? We have our own enemies in the UK, and some of them are rather stubborn when it comes to certain targets."

Ashley replied, "Because the League has way more dragon clans and dragon-shifters to keep track of here in the US, I think a short absence will help. As long as Lila leaves today and stays away for a little bit, I think they'll lose interest. As far as we know, there isn't any sort of international anti-dragon network that works together. Besides, the UK DDA sent you here for a trial, and I don't see why Lila can't do the same for ADDA, albeit as a human candidate instead of a dragon one. Especially *if* her brother is mated to a dragon-shifter."

Ashley looked pointedly at her, and Sylvia stiffened. Aye, she wanted Jake as her own, but not like this—not forced for merely the sake of protecting his family.

Because he would do anything for his sister, she was nearly sure of that.

And she wanted to help Lila too, but a small part of her wanted Jake to want her for her. Not because they merely had a child together. Or because his sister needed help.

Maybe that made her a selfish person, but she didn't want him to resent her for all he'd have to give up to be her mate. Because even once the threat was quelled back in Scotland, the choice would still be which dragon clan they would live on because of her and Sophie. Jake wouldn't be able to go back to the human world he was used to.

If she believed he loved her, Sylvia would risk it. However, he hadn't said anything and everything was still quite new.

Which made the odds of Jake learning to hate his life with her far greater.

It didn't matter that despite her best efforts not to

fall too quickly, Sylvia had realized she loved Jake the moment Finn had said the human had been flown back to America. She'd witnessed Logan's one-sided love for her daughter for years, and Sylvia wasn't going to sentence herself to the same.

Jake reached for her hand under the table and wrapped his warm fingers around her cold hand. Jake stated, "I'm going to talk to Sylvia alone. Can you two watch Sophie for a short while?"

Lila nodded and Ashley replied, "Of course. Cris is still outside, and she can take you to the other meeting room, one usually used for the Protectors."

Jake stood and tugged Sylvia up with him. She tried to smile but couldn't manage it. Instead, she blew a kiss at her daughter. "Mummy will be back soon, aye? Be good for your auntie."

And so she let Jake take her out of the room, ask for directions, and lead her to the other meeting room. All the while, her heart pounded in her chest, unsure of how their conversation would go.

For once, she was going to think like her dragon would—in other words, to not suspect the worst before it happened.

Although she was enough of a realist to know it might not go the way she wanted.

Still, she stood tall and followed her human. She'd taken a chance to come to America for Jake. That had taken more courage than she'd shown in a long while, if ever. She could remain strong for this too.

Sylvia wanted Jake to be hers desperately, but not at the risk of her heart and future happiness. It was time to be a wee bit more of the female she had always wanted to be and not settle for less than she was worth.

Chapter Twenty-One

J ake noticed the instant Sylvia paled and shuttered her gaze at Ashley's mention of mating.

Part of him wondered if she was afraid of taking another mate again. Or maybe she thought he would only mate her to protect his sister. She had so many reasons to want to say no.

Yet all he'd wanted to shout was yes, he wanted Sylvia as his own.

However, he held back. They had a rather unique relationship, one that had never really gone the usual way of things. And given his mistake in thinking someone had wanted to marry him before, only to betray him through dishonesty, Jake wanted to try to convince Sylvia of why he wanted to mate her more than anything. Lay out the truth for her and hope it was enough.

After all, he loved her, he loved their daughter, and after nearly a month without either, he knew with every bone in his body that he never wanted to be separated from his two dragon ladies ever again if he could help it.

Jake only needed to convince Sylvia of this. Which, of course, meant talking about Kim Gibbons —the woman he'd nearly married in his early twenties. That was the only way he could think of to argue how his love for Sylvia was different and special and more dear to him than his later realized infatuation with Kim.

Once they were inside the larger, nicer meeting room, he guided her to the small couch off to the side. He sat, and Sylvia did as well, removing her hand from his in the process.

And while he wanted to snatch it back, he resisted. Instead, he asked, "Talk to me, Sylvia, and tell me what's going on inside your head."

She met his gaze—he missed her flashing dragon eyes—but he couldn't read into her expression. "I want to say aye, I'll mate you. But…"

He raised his brows. "But?"

She sighed. "This is all happening so fast. It seems we come together, finally get into a routine, and then something happens to cause drama again." She bit her lip and he waited until she finally spoke again. "Not to mention things are still unsettled back in Scotland. And even if they weren't, and it's safe for you again, you'll have to give everything up if we live there. You know about my mum. I don't want that to happen to you too."

He did take her hand this time. "Honesty is what I want, and don't stop giving it to me. However, I hope you won't give up on us just yet."

She moved closer to him. "Of course not. I, well, just want some more time with you. To ensure it's what you truly want."

Reading between the lines, he wondered if it meant Sylvia *did* want to mate him.

Jake kissed her knuckles before replying, "And I completely understand that. I'm not going to pressure you. Although I do want to share a story with you, about how I can be more certain of you despite our short time together compared to the woman I dated for two years and had once thought to marry."

Her brows came together. "I vaguely remember you saying you were engaged before. But this is what I'm talking about, Jake. I should already know such an important part of your past."

Squeezing her hand, he smiled at her. "Well, then let's take one thing at a time and fix that, okay?" She nodded, and he reached up to tuck a section of hair behind her ear. "It was more than twenty years ago now…"

She tilted her head, waiting for him to continue, and Jake decided to just get it all out into the open. "Her name was Kimberly Gibbons. I met her at my first job after I finished culinary school. She helped her family with produce deliveries, and I saw her at least once a week and soon started dating her."

He'd once recalled Kim's face and figure perfectly. Now it was merely a blur. He went on, "We went out for two years and I thought I loved her. I couldn't seem to keep my hands off her, and I always tried to go out of my way to please her. In retrospect, I never noticed how she never said she loved me back. Nor did I really take seriously how she turned down my first two marriage proposals. However, I tried a third time on New Year's Eve when I was drunk, and she said yes."

He'd been so happy, even if the details had been hazy. Jake had never drunk as much as that fateful New Year's Eve.

Of course, if he'd been sober, he probably would've never asked Kim again in the first place. Mostly because he would've noticed her spending most of the party with someone else.

Pushing aside what he couldn't change, Jake continued, "She wanted a long engagement, which I didn't mind. We were both still young, after all, and we had to rely on ingenuity and hard work to put on the type of wedding she wanted.

"Then the day came." Even if it had been decades, Jake never forgot that day, or the humiliation that followed. "Even though Kim had never seemed quite as happy or enthusiastic about the wedding as me, I was still thrilled. I thought I was in love. I was finally going to start my own family and be as happy as my sisters were with their spouses. Except…"

Sylvia placed a hand on his thigh and squeezed. "Except what?"

He met her gaze again. "She never showed. Her friend gave me a letter, which said she'd run off with another man. It was later, once I could think again, that I learned her true aim. She'd had no intention of marrying me but had found someone else. However, she and this other guy decided that if she led me on, they could get a honeymoon for themselves, taking the one meant for me and Kim. Something they couldn't afford on their own."

Sylvia murmured something, but Jake carried on, needing to finish the tale. "To say I was devastated would be an understatement, not to mention the sting of betrayal. I had taken an extra job and extra shifts for nearly a year so I could pay for the wedding and the honeymoon. I would've done anything for her. And yet Kim apparently cared so little for me that she let me go on, not caring how exhausted I was, knowing full well she'd end up leaving and stealing from me." He grimaced. "Even though I'd been with her for years, I didn't know her at all. I decided shortly after being stood up that I was done with women. Without them, I could focus on my career, my dreams and never have to suffer another great disappointment again."

Jake cupped Sylvia's cheek and gazed deeply into her eyes. "But something about you was different, right from the beginning. You answered so forthrightly, even when your dragon's words clearly embarrassed you, and I couldn't help but wonder if maybe I'd found a woman who wouldn't try to lie and manipulate me."

She murmured, "And then I left you without a word in the night."

He stroked her skin. "Even that I could understand. We never promised anything between us, and you were a dragon-shifter and I was human, never an easy thing to begin with." He raised his other hand so he could take her face between them. "But don't you see, Sylvia? One day with you made more of an impression on me than nearly three years with the woman who betrayed me. To the point I had to find out why you left and to see if my gut instinct regarding women had improved over the last two decades." He leaned closer a fraction. "And it did. Talking with you is so easy. Even when you're afraid to share something that could paint you negatively, something you consider a dark part of your life, you still told me about it. You're more honest than most people I know." He laid his forehead against hers. "I know your history, some of your fears, your great love of your children, and how much you think of others' happiness. Not to mention how you show parts of yourself to me, such as the teasing, flirtatious woman, who rarely comes out for anyone else." He kissed her gently before whispering, "So even if the time has been short, I've never been more certain in my life of how much I love you, Sylvia. The question is—do you believe me?"

Jake had laid all his cards out on the table. Now all he could do was see how Sylvia reacted.

So his heart thumped and he held his breath, waiting for her answer.

Sylvia's heart hurt as Jake told her his tale. The thought of any female doing what they'd done to him, taking so clear advantage, made her want to find the female and wring out an apology.

And maybe growl and snap her teeth in her dragon form, just for good measure.

At the thought of protecting their male against someone who'd hurt him, her dragon stirred slightly but still didn't speak.

And then Jake had to go and lay out how much he knew of her, despite their short time together, melting away some of her fears.

By the time he said he loved her, Sylvia was doing her best not to cry. Not out of sadness, but a mixture of relief and happiness.

She, the female who fell in love too quickly by most standards, had somehow earned the love of her human.

So when he asked if she believed him, she nodded. "I do believe you. I tried to hold back, to keep myself from hoping for too much too quickly, but I've never been good at denying my feelings." She brushed some hair off his forehead, desperately needing to touch him, and smiled at her human. "And even if some would say it's too soon or that I'm vulnerable because of my silent dragon, they'd be wrong. I know with my whole heart that I love you, Jake Swift. I'd be a fool not to, given how sweet, funny, and loyal you are. Not to mention you can handle my children, which is no mean feat in and of itself."

He chuckled. "Your children are easy compared to your in-laws." He sobered a fraction before saying, "But even if our tale never went in the usual order of things up until now, I think maybe this once it'll be good to mate before we even think of another child, right?"

Her lips twitched. "Are you becoming all traditional now?"

He grinned. "Well, I don't want you running off, and a man's got to do what a man's got to do. Even if it means steering our relationship toward a more 'normal' path, I suppose."

He winked and she laughed. Jake cut it short by kissing her again, and she melted into him.

As his tongue stroked hers, his hand pulled her closer, his heat and scent wrapping around her, and Sylvia desperately wanted more than kissing, much more.

And yet somehow she remembered that even if they didn't have to worry about Sophie waking up or crying right this second, Jake's sister waited for them.

As if reading her thoughts, Jake broke the kiss and murmured, "You're thinking again, aren't you?"

She traced his bottom lip with her forefinger. "Aye, I can't help it. Although maybe once we finally have a somewhat boring, normal life, we can take a day or two away from Sophie to get all this pent-up lust out of our system with no distractions."

Jake's eyes turned heated. "I'll never get you out of my system, my dragon lady."

His words made her shiver in a good way. She heard the truth in them and believed him.

Sylvia traced his jaw, loving the feel of his short whiskers. "I doubt my dragon will tire of you, either."

He continued to rub her back, her shoulder, her arm, as if he needed to touch her or he'd die. "And yourself?"

The corner of her mouth ticked up. "We'll just have to see, aye? Dragon-shifters are a randy lot, after all."

"Oh, is that so?" He dragged her onto his lap and

tickled her side. She giggled and tried to stop him. Eventually he did and merely held her close. "I want you, Sylvia, more than anything. I want to be your mate, father and stepfather to your children, and somehow find a place within your clan."

She looked up from where her head rested on his shoulder. "Are you sure about that, Jake? Scotland is a long way from San Francisco."

He squeezed her hip. "I know. But I've spent the last twenty-odd years building up my career, my restaurants, and I've reached a place where I can step back a little and learn to delegate. And there's nowhere I'd rather do that from than on Lochguard with you, Sophie, and all your children."

"Even Connor?"

He snorted. "I can handle Connor."

As she imagined her son trying to win against Jake, she smiled. But then she remembered how that required them all to be back in Scotland, and her smile faded. "If we can ever go home."

He held her tighter against his chest. "You told me before to trust Finn, right? So let's trust him. Besides, there's something else we should worry about first."

She frowned up at him. "What?"

"If we mate on PineRock, will it hold up in Scotland? I have no idea if dragon-style marriages work like human ones, across borders."

"I don't know, but we should talk with Ashley and

find out." She bit her lip and then blurted, "Just as long as you're sure about this."

"Oh, I'm sure."

And then he kissed her possessively, exploring every inch of her mouth, letting her know with actions that he meant his words.

Well, for a few minutes, at least, before they both begrudgingly left the room and went to deal with Ashley and the next step toward their future.

Chapter Twenty-Two

Later that evening, after Lila had left and been escorted to the airport—she'd go home, pack, and be ready to leave for a vacation with her children —Jake was in bed with Sylvia half laying on his chest, stroking her bare back in slow circles.

Since Jamie, Ashley, and Wes had all volunteered to watch Sophie for a night to give Jake and Sylvia a chance to be alone, they hadn't wasted time tearing each other's clothes off and showing how much they'd missed each other.

But as much as Jake loved sex with Sylvia, he felt more content merely holding her, knowing she was his and would be forever.

Well, as soon as they could schedule a mating ceremony, that was.

Hugging her closer to his side, he reveled in his dragon lady nuzzling his chest. She was the first to speak. "There's one thing I haven't told you yet, about what Finn and the others found out during their investigation into Arlo."

Jake never stilled his hands. "Tell me, love."

She propped her chin on his chest and looked up, meeting his gaze. "Arlo set up Arthur's friend's death, laying a trap in exchange for money."

He searched her gaze. "Was Arthur the original target?"

"No one knows. But the spot Arthur mentioned searching, the one he said was somewhere he'd met his friends as a child and teen, was one all of the MacAllister siblings seemed to know about—Seamus told me that. So it's likely that once the opportunity finally arose to get rid of Arthur, Arlo would've taken it."

He brushed hair off Sylvia's cheek, wishing he could banish the sadness in her eyes. "I'm not sure anything I say can help you. But at least Arlo won't ever endanger someone you love again."

She ran a hand through his chest hair, and Jake did his best to ignore the sizzle of heat that shot to his groin. Sylvia answered, "No, he won't." She paused, bit her lip, and then finally added, "As nice as everyone is here, I hope we can return to Lochguard soon."

He hugged her closer to his body. "You miss your children."

"Aye, I can't help it. I know they're grown, but,

well, they've been my only family for so long that it's difficult to sever ties completely. I can't imagine what it's going to be like for you, if we can ever live on Lochguard, and you have to do the same with everyone here in the States."

He rolled until he lay on his side, facing Sylvia, meeting her eye to eye. He hated how she still doubted him. But given her past with her mother, he knew it would take some reassurance for a while to make sure she truly understood his decision.

Taking one of her hands, he threaded his fingers through hers and squeezed. "I love my sisters and their families, but they're each their own little unit, banding together and understanding one another far better than I ever could. It's not the same at all compared to you being away from your kids." He traced her cheek with his free hand, loving how she turned into his touch. "Besides, Lochguard is Sophie's home. She deserves to know her siblings, even if they'll end up being more like aunts and uncles to her because of the age difference."

Sylvia smiled. "I suspect my granddaughter— Sophie's niece—will feel more like a cousin or a sibling, probably more so than Sophie's own older siblings."

He chuckled. "Your family tree will never be boring, that's for sure."

She cupped his cheek with her hand, and he turned to kiss her palm before she said, "Well, since there will soon be an American human branch, aye, it's going to be a wee bit more interesting than most. But I wouldn't have it any other way." She lifted her head to kiss him gently and murmur, "You've brought me a second chance at life, at love, and motherhood. I can't wait to see what other sorts of surprises show up along the way."

He gently took her other hand, rolled Sylvia to her back, and pinned both of her arms above her head. "As for surprises, I'm still working on the cheesiest pick-up line ever." He nipped her jaw before adding, "Let's see…are you Australian? Because you meet all of my koala-fications."

She snorted, and he took her lips in a rough kiss, loving how Sylvia instantly opened her mouth and stroked her tongue against his.

He maneuvered so he held both of her hands with one of his own. Using his free hand, he ran it down her neck, her chest, and finally he circled her already hard nipple, loving how Sylvia arched against him as he slowly stroked, taking his time with his dragon lady, letting her know that he wasn't going anywhere and had all the time in the world to treasure her as she deserved.

Leaning down, he licked her tight bud and watched as her pupils flashed for the first time since arriving on PineRock. With a chuckle, he moved his face back to hers and asked, "What did your dragon say?"

A mischievous gleam filled Sylvia's eyes. "That she wants the chance to say hello properly."

Sliding his hand down between her thighs, he lightly ran a finger through her slit until he reached her hard little clit and pressed down. Sylvia's pupils changed to slits for a beat longer this time before becoming round again. "And now?"

"I think showing you would be more fun."

And before he could ask anything else, Sylvia flipped them until he was on his back and she straddled his hips. With her wet, hot heat against his skin, his cock turned to stone. When she wiggled her hips, he groaned. "Are you going to keep me pinned and torture me until I beg?"

Leaning down, she nipped his bottom lip before saying, "I'm tempted, but my dragon is impatient. Now, stay here and don't move."

She rolled over, took a condom package from the nightstand, opened it, and rolled it down his cock slowly, to the point he was afraid he'd spill like a horny teenager with his first time.

She stroked his upper thighs, up his stomach, and stopped to lightly run her nails over his nipples and back again. He reached for her, but her eyes flashed and she took his hands and pinned them to the side.

As Sylvia half leaned over him, her lovely breasts swaying in front of him, he tried to lean up to kiss one. But she angled back with a smile. "Later. My beast and I don't want slow and torturous." Releasing his hands, she raised herself over his cock and slid down. He moaned at how wet and hot she was, and he arched his hips, desperately wanting her to move.

Sylvia placed her hands on his chest and rocked her hips. With his hands free, Jake caressed her hips, her sides, and then cupped her breasts. She arched into his touch and increased her motions, making Jake bite his cheek to keep from coming right away.

He wondered if he'd always be like this with his dragon lady, and he had a feeling he could be sixty and she could make him come so very easily. Her spell over him was unlike that of any other woman he'd ever met.

Sylvia whispered, "I love you," before her pupils turned to slits and stayed that way. Her voice was a tad deeper, meaning her dragon was in charge, as she added, "And now you're mine."

She lightly dug her nails into his chest, the pleasure-pain making him call out her name. Then her dragon moved faster and faster, to the point Jake had to hold her hips to ground him.

Since he loved all of Sylvia, he'd missed her beast. And even though she currently drove him mad with her hip swirls and faster thrusts, he somehow managed to move a hand to her clit and stroke. Within seconds, he felt her pussy clench and release him, and Jake finally let go, calling her name as her dragon-half dug her nails harder into his chest.

When she finally collapsed on top of him, he

instinctively knew the human half was back with him. Hugging Sylvia tighter against his body, he said, "I'm glad she's back. I love all of you, and it was rather lonely without your dragon around."

Sylvia turned her head and smiled at him. "You just miss her quick and rough bedplay."

He rubbed circles on her ass cheek before squeezing possessively. "Oh, I won't deny I love that. But even now, with your human half front and center, I can tell you're more content, and not just from your orgasm. You need her present in order to be the woman I first met back in Glasgow."

She brushed some hair off his forehead. "You understand dragon-shifters so well."

He lightly smacked her butt. "Well, I did fall in love with one. I hope I know something, or life would be full of a hell of a lot of surprises."

"Oh, I'm sure there are plenty of surprises ahead." For a beat, sadness flashed in her eyes—no doubt Sylvia wondering if she'd have to make a new life in America—but it vanished and was replaced by love. "But as long as you're there with me, I can face any sort of surprise that comes our way. You give me strength I thought I'd lost, or always thought I never had."

He squeezed her tighter against him. "I have a feeling it was always there, but sometimes we need something or someone to help nurture it out." He kissed her gently. "When we get back to Lochguard,

I'm sure Meg or Archie will think twice before trying to bully or guilt-trip you into agreeing to what they want."

A mischievous glint appeared in Sylvia's eyes. "I may need a wee bit more tutelage in American cockiness."

He nipped her jaw. "You mean confidence."

Her smile was so bright, his heart skipped a beat. "No, definitely cockiness."

He growled, "I think I need to use something other than words to try and change your mind. And I'm confident enough I can do it."

He flipped her over to her back, tickled her until she couldn't stop giggling, and she finally conceded it was confidence. And then, unable to resist Sylvia's flushed cheeks and happy smiles, Jake made love to her again slowly, until she begged for him to make her come.

He'd been more than happy to make that happen. Jake would do anything for Sylvia—he already thought of her as his wife and mate, even if they'd agreed to wait to officially mate until they had word from Finn and Lochguard.

But just to make sure she understood his claim on her, he made her scream his name two more times before drifting off to sleep with his dragon lady cradled in his arms.

Chapter Twenty-Three

I ris Mahajan had spent the last six weeks tapping every source she had, calling in a few favors, and finally spending every waking moment trying to determine who inside Lochguard had worked with Arlo MacAllister.

The blasted report from Antony's people had said there were two suspected accomplices in the illegal dragon's blood operation, one of whom at least lived on Lochguard themselves.

Which was why she was now dressed in a bloody impractical skirt and top, with a cardigan to cover her dragon-shifter tattoo, doing her best to blend in on the busy Royal Mile in Edinburgh, waiting for her suspect to show his face.

She was almost positive that Lance MacCann had a meeting in the next half hour along the Mile, although she wasn't quite sure of where.

Despite Lance's mate, Harriet, being the daughter of Lochguard's old clan leader—the old male had used fear to rule and rarely had dealt with clan issues unless bloodshed was imminent—the female was sweet and didn't have a dishonest bone in her body. Harriet was friends with Kiyana Boyd and Gina MacDonald-MacKenzie, two of the human females living on Lochguard.

And since Gina's mate, Fergus, helped gather intelligence for Lochguard, Iris had trusted him to help her keep track of information. According to Fergus, Harriet had said Lance was going to be out of town for the day to supposedly meet some local schoolteachers about doing a cross-cultural event for human and dragon children.

On the surface, it seemed plausible. Lance's mate worked part-time at the school, and the female always wanted to find new ways to introduce the dragon children, including her own, to human ones.

However, Lance had merely requested permission to visit Edinburgh to do some shopping. Or so the paperwork Finn had shown her said.

Iris had caught Lance in the lie, and Finn trusted her enough to let her see where it went. As of late, Lance had earned some rather large commissions for his website and social media strategy consultations, far beyond what he'd ever earned in the past. And some digging had revealed no recently acquired big clients either.

It was the extra income, plus the lie, that made Iris's gut scream Lance was her target.

Her dragon huffed but remained silent. Iris bit back a smile, knowing how hard it was for her beast to do so. But they were in Edinburgh in broad daylight so she'd never pass for human if her pupils started flashing.

Especially since it was a gloomy day and sunglasses would seem out of place.

Iris quickly checked her phone, but there were no messages from Brodie or Cooper. They were also Lochguard Protectors. Brodie she'd trained with back in the British Army, and Cooper was Lochguard's second-in-command of security. She trusted both of them with her life.

And since she couldn't watch the entire mile herself—even with certain establishments banning dragon-shifters from entering, narrowing down Lance's destination choices—she needed Brodie and Cooper's help to watch the other end, closer to the Palace of Holyroodhouse, as well as the middle section. Iris was keeping watch closer to Edinburgh Castle.

As she continued to simultaneously browse the wares outside the tacky souvenir shop and watch the street for signs of Lance, something across the way caught her attention. A broad-shouldered figure, dressed in an unremarkable dark suit, sat at the window of a cafe, drinking tea and pretending to read a newspaper.

Aye, pretending because he currently stared straight at her and winked.

It was that bloody human, Antony Holbrook.

What the hell was he doing here?

Her dragon wanted to speak but couldn't. What Iris wouldn't give for some sunshine and a pair of sunglasses.

But even without her dragon's words, Iris could guess why the male was here. Either Antony had been watching her since the whole mess with Jake Swift, or he had information confirming what she'd suspected, in that Lance MacCann was indeed the inside traitor on Lochguard.

The first option was merely annoying. The second pissed her off.

She'd worked hard to piece together information and get herself to Edinburgh, all whilst never letting on she was a dragon-shifter.

And if that damn human male ruined it, she was tempted to lure him somewhere isolated and show just how accomplished she was at taking a human down.

Aye, he could do with a bit of humility, that was for sure.

Her dragon laughed, but Iris ignored her beast. No doubt her dragon would think of another way to deal with him, one that involved no clothes and a bed.

But no matter how attractive he might be, she wasn't going to allow him to undermine her. Iris had devoted her life to becoming a Protector, to protect the clan that had welcomed her parents when some of the other British clans had turned up their noses at taking them in decades ago.

Lochguard was hers to protect, not his.

Then she noticed a familiar tall male form walking down the street with his head bent and the collar of his jacket turned up high.

The brown-haired form of Lance MacCann had finally shown up, bringing her mind back to focus on her task.

As Lance eventually entered a pub down the street, Iris slowly made her way toward it too.

When she crossed the street, she quickly glanced toward the cafe. Antony was gone.

She resisted a growl. He was going to swoop in and take credit for her work.

Maybe to some it wouldn't matter, as long as the guilty were taken into custody and dealt with.

However, Iris had had enough of males swooping in to take credit for her work during her time in the army or during the annual training exercises most Protectors had to attend with the British Army, Royal Navy, and Royal Air Force members.

Cocky human males who thought they were so much better than her.

Not only because she was female, but also

because her parents were from India, which somehow made her less everything—competent, intelligent, brave, trustworthy, and the list went on.

Pushing aside the memories of the arseholes from her time in the army and a few times since, she focused on slipping inside the pub and blending into the background. All that mattered was getting the evidence she needed to convict Lance and rid Lochguard of its latest threat. Only then could Sylvia MacAllister come home with the male she seemed to fancy.

Quickly scanning the room, Iris didn't spot Lance anywhere. However, she noted the stairs toward the back of the place.

After quickly ordering a soda—any sort of alcohol purchases by a dragon-shifter in Edinburgh could lead to trouble if reported—she went upstairs.

Since it was near lunchtime, the place was mostly filled with tourists enjoying the regular pub fare of fish and chips, meat pies, and burgers. In the far corner, away from the window, she spotted Lance sitting at a table.

Not just Lance—no, he was sitting across from Antony.

For a beat she wondered if she'd misjudged either of the males, but quickly ignored it. Too many lies and unaccounted monies said Lance was up to something he shouldn't be.

But whereas Lance didn't know Iris was there,

Antony did. And the human male could easily destroy all her hard work with a sentence or two.

Mentally cursing Antony Holbrook, she slid into a chair at a small table along one wall and did her best to inconspicuously watch them while pretending to do something on her phone.

In less than five minutes Lance left, never noticing Iris off to the side.

However, Antony casually walked by her table, dropping a napkin on his way, all while never looking at her.

Unfolding the crumpled napkin, she read the message: *Old Assembly Close, birdbath. 20 minutes. Tell no one.*

The human wanted a meeting, did he?

She quickly looked up the location of the specified close on her phone—there were heaps of the small alleys along the Royal Mile—and discovered it wasn't far from the famous St. Giles Cathedral just down the road.

Hmm. Iris didn't like meeting Antony alone without telling anyone, but she had a way around that. She quickly typed up and scheduled an email to go out to Brodie and Cooper in an hour. That way, if something happened to her, they'd know where to start looking.

In the meantime, she'd see what he had to say.

Quickly finishing her soda, Iris exited the pub and casually walked down the street. The best way to go around a human city without anyone realizing she was a dragon-shifter was to act like one of the tourists.

So even though she hated wasting time buying a postcard and stopping a few times to look at T-shirts and tartan blankets, she reached the close before the deadline. She didn't know exactly where the birdbath was at, the narrow alley off the main street wasn't long, and she noticed Antony standing next to a little outcrop building with some sort of warning sign on the green door. The fence created a little area surrounded by trees and a birdbath on one side and the building on the other.

Since people were walking down the close and through the small courtyard to the left of the birdbath, she'd have to be careful and not let her eyes flash or talk too loud.

No doubt Antony had planned that.

If he wasn't interfering in her own investigation, she might acknowledge admiring him a wee bit.

But no, there were more important things to worry about.

She approached him, trying her best not to notice how his hair was a touch too long or how his shoes were a wee bit scuffed. All part of his cover, she imagined.

Not that she thought his broad shoulders or narrow waist were part of it; he probably ran triathlons for fun, to prove he could win over those younger than him. Aye, she could see that, for sure.

Although she had to admit that he was fit for his age. Maybe too fit.

Pushing aside any thoughts about what Antony might look like under his clothes, she stopped a foot away from him and merely raised her brows. The human smiled. "Good afternoon to you, too, my dear."

Again with his little endearments. But Iris wouldn't let it get to her, not here. Keeping her voice low, she said, "The bigger question is: Why were you meeting him? I'm beginning to think that maybe you're not on our side but merely on your own."

He brushed some imaginary dirt off his sleeve. The male tried too hard to appear nonchalant, that was for sure. He replied, "I owe too much to a dragon-shifter to ever hurt them. But do you want to waste time discussing me or our mutual acquaintance?"

No doubt his words about owing a dragon-shifter were merely to throw her off and distract her. "The mutual acquaintance you just had a drink with?"

"More like who just admitted to his crimes without even knowing it."

She narrowed her eyes. "He may not be the cleverest male alive, but surely he wouldn't trust you so easily."

"Ah, but this isn't the first time he and I have

met." He leaned closer, and Iris ignored the heat rolling off his body. "I've been working on this for a while, my dear. Although it's nice for you to have finally caught up."

She clenched her jaw and resisted making a fist. Something about this human made her want to slap or punch him.

Her dragon laughed but still remained silent. For once, Iris was glad her beast couldn't talk right now and fluster her further. "Do you have a point? Otherwise I'm going to leave."

He raised one brown eyebrow. Unlike his hair, it didn't have any gray yet. "We both know you're lying. Unless you want to scurry back, tail between your legs, and admit defeat. Or you can stay and I can share what I learned. Either way, your pest won't be a problem much longer. The only question is whether you want to tell your *boss* what happened or have him hear it from me."

She hated the vague conversation, but the mention of her boss referred to her clan leader.

Still, his tone was bloody irritating. This human male was entirely too comfortable being in charge and being obeyed without question.

Too bad she couldn't call him out on it. Only because of the people milling about did Iris keep her voice low. "What did you find out?"

"See? It's not that hard to be civil." At the humor in his eyes, she did make a fist but refrained from hitting him. As if sensing he was about to go too far, he continued, "The acquaintance is guilty." He leaned even closer, his hot breath dancing across her ear as he said, "He'll be making the exchange in a few hours. Once he does, my people will take him into custody. JS should be safe enough to return after that, with the threats to his life gone."

JS had to mean Jake Swift.

Iris grunted. "I want a detailed report. It could help me keep an eye out for future problems."

He leaned back and searched her gaze, a beat longer than was proper.

Her dragon swished her tail inside Iris's mind, no doubt wanting to say something about the deep brown depths or firm lips that she couldn't tell if they were warm or cold.

Pushing aside her dragon's radiating lust, she waited for Antony's answer. Once she had it, she could walk away and hopefully never have to see him again.

Aye, then she could focus back on improving her tracking and spying skills to better protect her clan. Her few interactions with Antony had taught her she still had a lot to learn.

He smiled slowly, and Iris ignored how it made him appear years younger than he was. Antony finally spoke again. "I'll send you a private report, one for your eyes only. Maybe you'll learn something from it, so next time I don't have to swoop in and help."

Iris rarely lost her temper, but this male was pushing it ever closer to bursting. Through clenched teeth, she said, "Fine. I'm leaving now."

She turned to leave, but Antony took hold of her wrist. Ignoring how his long fingers almost made her feel dainty, she glared at him. "What?"

"We'll meet again, my dear. Never fear."

He released her and Iris turned and walked away.

Part of her hoped he was lying and she'd never set eyes on him again.

And yet another part was eager for it, making her heart thump inside her chest. Not only could he teach her a few things—loath as she was to admit it —she wanted to poke and prod until he lost his nonchalant mask.

Because aye, it was a mask. And who knew what lay beneath.

Taking out her phone, she erased her scheduled email and sent messages to Brodie and Cooper about meeting up and returning to Lochguard.

All that mattered in the end was how her clan was safe. At least for the time being.

Chapter Twenty-Four

After staying nearly a month together on PineRock, Sylvia and Jake had finally been allowed to return back to Lochguard.

Saying goodbye to Wes and Ashley had been harder than Sylvia had thought it would be, but she was determined to get the pair to Scotland at some point. Not just because Finn wanted to better know the American clan leader, but because they were part of Jake's family, and she wanted to welcome any and all of his family she could.

Her dragon spoke up. *Most of them are already here and waiting in the great hall. They should've come to fetch us already.*

She and Jake had agreed that they wouldn't hold their mating ceremony until her dragon had returned after their flight back to Scotland, which had happened two days ago. *Patience, dragon.*

Why? I've wanted him for more than a year. Everyone needs to know he's ours.

I somehow don't think that's in doubt.

And not just because she and Jake had a daughter together, either. All of her older children had teased endlessly about them being smitten with one another. Well, except for Jamie. He was still sulking over having to come back to Scotland. Sylvia wondered if he'd felt more at home on PineRock without all his siblings, but she hadn't had time to talk to her son about it yet.

However, Arabella MacLeod—Finn's mate—entered the small room, smiled at her, and garnered Sylvia's attention. "Everything's ready if you are."

Jake's sisters had wanted a blended ceremony, a little of a human wedding combined with the traditional dragon-shifter attire, vows, and mating bands. The result meant a lot of quick work to get it all done in time.

None of which Sylvia had been allowed to see since it was supposed to be a surprise.

She took up the bouquet her soon-to-be sisters-in-law had given her—soft pink roses, chrysanthemums, and carnations with some bits of greenery she couldn't name—and nodded. "Aye, then let's not delay any longer."

Arabella touched her arm. "I'm so glad it worked out with Jake. I rather like him, although don't tell Finn or he'll get jealous for no reason."

Given the way Finn and Arabella looked at each other all the time—as if they each held the sun in their eyes and would wither without it—she barely resisted a snort at the idea of Finn being jealous over Jake.

Although her dragon grumbled, *He's* ours.

Aye, of course. Now, hush and calm down.

"Me too, Ara. Me too."

With a nod, Arabella exited, and Sylvia followed down the small hallway that led to one of the main doors into the massive hall. Unlike with a traditional dragon-shifter ceremony when she'd merely go to the dais from a side door, Sylvia was going to walk up toward the front, where Jake would be waiting, apparently like they did with human weddings.

In a way, she was happy for the slightly unusual wedding-slash-mating ceremony. It honored her love for Jake in a different way than the love she'd held for Arthur.

And even if her first mate was no longer around, Sylvia liked to think the bright sunshine streaming in through the windows was Arthur's doing, as if he approved of her finding happiness again.

She mentally whispered, *I'll always love and miss you, Arthur. But don't worry, Jake will take good care of me, I promise.*

Finn appeared. Since Sylvia's father had died long ago, he'd offered to walk her down the aisle in the human fashion instead. He held out his arm. "Ready, lass?"

She couldn't help but smile at Finn's words, given he was younger than her and she was no longer a lassie. "Aye. More than ready."

He winked at her. "Good. Then let's not keep them waiting any longer, or Jake's sisters may hunt me down and herd us up the aisle, nipping our heels to make us go faster."

She bit her lip to keep from laughing. Lila and Ada really had taken over the great hall for days, convincing everyone to help them give their baby brother the ceremony he deserved. Nearly everyone on Lochguard said they rivaled dragon-shifters for their confidence and dominance when barking orders.

But then music filtered into the air, and the doors to the great hall opened, and Sylvia forgot about everything but the male standing up on the raised dais, staring at her with eyes full of love and happiness.

JAKE HAD ARGUED with his sisters about delaying his mating ceremony with Sylvia so they could decorate the hall. None of that had mattered to him, only that he wanted to claim Sylvia as his mate in front of all.

But as Sylvia finally made her way up the aisle

created by people standing to either side of the opening, he forgot about everything but the beautiful dragonwoman walking toward him.

Dressed in the simple dark blue gown worn by dragon-shifters, knotted over one shoulder, and her dark hair gathered up to the back of her head with a few tendrils around her face, he wondered if she'd always continue to find ways of being more beautiful to him.

Her shy smile only made him want to meet her halfway, but he held his place. He learned a little more every day about how to balance between allowing Sylvia to handle things on her own and when he needed to step in.

This was one of the times she could handle herself, even if being the center of attention wasn't where she longed to be. She was doing it to please his sisters, and he couldn't love her more for it if he tried.

Once they climbed the stairs to the dais and reached him, Finn handed her over to Jake, issuing some threat or another that he didn't hear. No, Jake only had eyes and ears for Sylvia, itching to kiss her already and take her home.

The music died down, and she shifted her bouquet to one hand so she could pick up the silver armband engraved with her name in the old dragon language. Even if the decorations and start were in the human wedding fashion, the ceremony itself would be pure dragon-shifter.

As such, Sylvia would go first to help him understand how to do it. She cleared her throat and spoke loudly. "When we first met, over a year ago, I thought I was dying and had been so determined to be the person I always wanted to be, so much so that I dared to flirt and more with a human I'd just met. Even if we parted after a day, you gifted me with our darling Sophie. But even as much as I loved our daughter, something was always missing. And then you showed up on Lochguard, and it was as if the missing piece had arrived. Sophie adored you from the first day, and even if I didn't think I'd get to keep you, you made me laugh and offered support I didn't realize I needed.

"Plenty of things tried to tear us apart since then, and our courtship spanned two continents. But it was all worth it, every tear or worry, because I love you, Jake Swift. You bring out a side of me I needed, one that said it was okay to love again and be myself after losing my first mate. I stake my claim on you. Do you accept?"

"I do."

She slipped the band over his bicep—he was also in traditional dragon garb, with a kilt-like outfit that left his arms and most of his chest bare—and then she smiled up at him, letting him know it was his turn.

Jake plucked the remaining armband up, a smaller version of the one on his arm, except the engraving was of his name in the old dragon language. Never taking his gaze from Sylvia's, he said, "If I'm honest, I never thought I'd be a father or want to get married at this stage of my life. I focused on work, wanting to forget the past. But then you showed up in my life, a breath of honesty and sweetness I couldn't ignore if I wanted to. One night was never enough, and even though it took longer than I'd wanted, I finally found you again and discovered the truth of not only our daughter but the fact you had five other kids, who are more protective than I really like." A few chuckles rolled through the room, and Jake continued, "But not even being threatened by your sons, or even kidnapped by a dragon-shifter, was enough to drive me away. When you showed up in the US, I thought I had to be dreaming. But you were real, and I vowed to never let you go again. I love you, Sylvia. You bring a softness and lightness to my life I didn't think could exist. And I hope we can grow old together, laughing and loving one another without any other big surprises. However, if they do show up, we'll face them together, no matter what it takes. I stake my claim on you. Do you accept?"

"Aye."

He slipped the silver around the arm without her

dragon-shifter tattoo and finally drew her close and kissed her.

Sylvia had suggested a quick peck, but he held her closer, parted her lips, and devoured her mouth as if it were the first or last time.

Eventually someone's throat clearing made him break the kiss, and he spotted Finn grinning at him. "Aye, there's plenty of time for that later. For now, let's celebrate Jake and Sylvia!"

Cheers rose and Sylvia melted into his side for a few beats before they did their duty and went to accept all the congratulations from the clan members.

They finished with Sylvia's kids, his sisters, and Sophie. Jake took his daughter from Lila and kissed her cheek. "How about we dance with your mommy to celebrate?"

Sophie merely plucked at the material across his chest.

Connor snorted. "Careful, or she'll have you undressed in the middle of the great hall."

Sylvia took Sophie and whispered a bit loudly, "No undressing Daddy in public. He's not used to it yet." Sylvia met his gaze. "But trust me, I'm working on it. Otherwise he'll have you shredding a new set of clothes every time you shift."

He drew Sylvia to his side and placed a hand over hers holding Sophie. "We'll worry about that in five or six years. For now, I just want to dance with my two dragon ladies."

Not waiting to hear what his sisters or his stepkids said, Jake guided them to the square set aside for dancing. It was a bit awkward, but he drew Sylvia, holding Sophie, closer and began waltzing them around the space.

And even though he was counting down the minutes until he could claim his new mate, Jake was content to hold his wife and daughter close, dancing with them, and wondering if anyone could die of love and happiness.

But if so, it was a challenge he'd gladly look forward to.

Epilogue

A Little Over a Year Later

Sylvia watched as Connor dished out the last of the special meal they'd made into a large dish, and she directed her other four older children to carry all of the plates and bowls filled with food outside.

As she was extremely pregnant with her seventh —and final since Jake was getting a vasectomy— child, no one would let her do anything. Which had been nice at first, but it had grown to ridiculous proportions.

Her dragon laughed. *You know they're just worried about you.*

I know, but I'm a pro at this by now. You think they'd trust me.

They do. But Jake missed the time we were pregnant with Sophie, and I think he's making up for it.

Sylvia suspected it as well, which was the only reason she didn't let her temper loose more often. *Just another two months and this will be over. As much as I love my children, I look forward to the never being pregnant again part.*

Her beast laughed just as Jake walked in, pulled her close, and kissed her. "Talking with your dragon about me behind my back?"

Her lips twitched. "Aye, maybe."

He kissed her and then lightly smacked her bum. "You know she always ends up on my side, though."

She raised an eyebrow. "Not always."

He grinned. "I know. She wants me to always walk around without any clothes on. But that's one I'm standing firm on."

Her beast grumbled and Sylvia laughed. "She'll wear you down eventually."

He opened his mouth to reply, but their unborn wee one did a tumble and kicked. Since Jake was up against her belly, he felt it and put his hand over the spot. "Are you trying to tell your mom and dad to cut it out? If so, you're going to be doing that your whole life."

Sylvia placed her hand over his. Even though dragon-shifters traditionally waited until the birth to find out the gender, Jake had worn her down, eager to prepare for his second child. She said, "No doubt she'll team up with her sister and create a united front against us."

"If I can handle my five stepchildren, plus a few of their mates, as well as our daughter, I think I can handle one more."

"Aye, maybe. But there could be another mate to add to the crowd before long, given how Ian keeps avoiding your niece above everyone else."

Jake frowned. "Are you sure he didn't say if she's his true mate or not?"

She shook her head. "Ian's the quiet one and keeps more to himself. And believe me, if Emma can't get it out of him, no one can. Not even being his twin is enough to crack him."

Jake grunted. "Well, I'll just watch the pair closely. This is only the second time my nieces and nephew have really interacted with dragon-shifters— not since our wedding—and not all of them are as comfortable as I am. Maybe she's merely avoiding him."

Sylvia leaned against him. "They'll be fine, I'm sure. Speaking of which, we should go outside to join them and the others. After spending the day hiking and swimming, I'm sure everyone's famished. And when my children are hungry, they pick fights. And I'd rather save us all from that."

Jake chuckled before turning her toward him again and cupping her cheek. "In a minute. I need a little taste of my mate before dealing with that crowd again."

She smiled as he took her lips in a deep, searching kiss, making her moan and grip onto him. Her belly made it harder to kiss him like this, but they somehow managed.

And as Jake lay claim to her mouth, showing her that he loved her even more than before, Sylvia sighed and wondered for the thousandth time how she'd been lucky to find love twice in her life.

But then Jake turned their kiss into a bit more, whisking her to a side room and making her come with his fingers, and she simply embraced her happiness with the one-night stand that had ended up stealing her heart forever.

Author's Note

Thanks for reading Jake and Sylvia's story! This one was difficult for many reasons, the foremost being that Sylvia's personality is so very different from mine and I had the devil of a time writing her. But in the end, I think it turned out well. And let's just say that steamy scenes with a nursing mother is another difficulty, and one I hope I don't have to do again for a while. (I've done two this year—this book and *The Survivor* in my Kelderan Runic Warriors series. Sigh to the lack of more nipple play…oops, did I just say that?) Of course you'll see Jake and Sylvia pop up in future books since I have four more MacAllisters (the older ones) to write stories for. :)

This book also set up a few stories. Besides a little more on Connor and Aimee, you also got a peek at Logan and Emma, as well as Iris and Antony. And while a lot of people wanted Iris to be with Max, they just don't fit and never really have. (Max has his own Aussie dragon lady love to worry about, once she stops stealing all his dig sites, of course.) Max's older brother, on the other hand, is perfect for Iris in so many ways. I'm very much looking forward to the May-December story of theirs, for sure. Logan and Emma's story should be fun and emotional as well, and is next in the Lochguard series. At the moment the release order for these are: 1) Logan & Emma, 2) Iris & Antony, and 3) Aimee & Connor (unless Ian's story demands to be before his brother's).

And I'll also hint that there is more to Katrina Lau than you know. (She worked with Antony in this story, remember.) The truth of her identity will surprise you, and lead to a story of her own. But that is news for another day….

Curious yet?

And now, I have some people to thank for getting this out in the world:

- To Becky Johnson and her team at Hot Tree Editing. They always catch the little things and Becky helps keep my British characters sounding, well, British, LOL.
- To all my beta readers—Sabrina D.,

Donna H., Sandy H., and Iliana G., you do an amazing job at finding those lingering typos and minor inconsistencies.

And as always, a huge thank you to you, the reader, for sticking with me. Writing is the best job in the world and it's your support that makes it so I can keep doing it. If you've read the books and want to support me in another way, almost all of my dragon-shifter audiobooks either are, or will be soon, available in libraries around the globe. Take a listen and enjoy some lovely accents!

Until next time, happy reading!

PS—To keep up-to-date with new releases and other goodies, please join my newsletter on my website: www.JessieDonovan.com

The Dragon's Choice

TAHOE DRAGON MATES #1

After Jose Santos's younger sister secretly enters them both into the yearly dragon lottery and they get selected, he begrudgingly agrees to participate. It means picking a human female from a giant room full of them and staying around just long enough to get her pregnant. However, when his dragon notices one female who keeps hiding behind a book, Jose has a new plan—win his fated mate, no matter what it takes.

Victoria Lewis prefers being home with a book and away from large crowds. But she desperately wants to study dragon-shifters at close range, so she musters up her courage to enter the dragon lottery. When she's selected as one of the potential candidates, she decides to accept her spot. After all, it's not as if the dragon-shifter will pick her—an introverted bookworm who prefers jeans and sweats to skirts or fancy clothes. Well, until he's standing right in front of her with flashing eyes and says he wants her.

As Jose tries to win his fated female, trouble stirs inside his clan. Will he be able to keep his mate with him forever? Or will the American Department of Dragon Affairs whisk her away to some other clan to protect her?

The Dragon's Choice is now available in paperback.

Also by Jessie Donovan

Asylums for Magical Threats

Blaze of Secrets (AMT #1)

Frozen Desires (AMT #2)

Shadow of Temptation (AMT #3)

Flare of Promise (AMT #4)

Cascade Shifters

Convincing the Cougar (CS #0.5)

Reclaiming the Wolf (CS #1)

Cougar's First Christmas (CS #2)

Resisting the Cougar (CS #3)

Dragon Clan Gatherings

Summer at Lochguard (DCG #1 / Nov 4, 2021)

Kelderan Runic Warriors

The Conquest (KRW #1)

The Barren (KRW #2)

The Heir (KRW #3)

The Forbidden (KRW #4)

The Hidden (KRW #5)

The Survivor (KRW #6)

Lochguard Highland Dragons

The Dragon's Dilemma (LHD #1)

The Dragon Guardian (LHD #2)

The Dragon's Heart (LHD #3)

The Dragon Warrior (LHD #4)

The Dragon Family (LHD #5)

The Dragon's Discovery (LHD #6)

The Dragon's Pursuit (LHD #7)

The Dragon Collective (LHD #8)

The Dragon's Chance (LHD #9)

The Dragon's Memory / Logan & Emma (LHD #10 / May 5, 2022)

Love in Scotland

Crazy Scottish Love (LiS #1)

Chaotic Scottish Wedding (LiS #2)

Stonefire Dragons

Sacrificed to the Dragon (SD #1)

Seducing the Dragon (SD #2)

Revealing the Dragons (SD #3)

Healed by the Dragon (SD #4)

Reawakening the Dragon (SD #5)

Loved by the Dragon (SD #6)

Surrendering to the Dragon (SD #7)

Cured by the Dragon (SD #8)

Aiding the Dragon (SD #9)

Finding the Dragon (SD #10)

Craved by the Dragon (SD #11)

Persuading the Dragon (SD #12)

Treasured by the Dragon (SD #13)

Trusting the Dragon / Hudson & Sarah (SD #14, Jan 20, 2022)

Stonefire Dragons Shorts

Meeting the Humans (SDS #1)

The Dragon Camp (SDS #2)

The Dragon Play (SDS #3)

Stonefire Dragons Universe

Winning Skyhunter (SDU #1)

Transforming Snowridge (SDU #2)

Tahoe Dragon Mates

The Dragon's Choice (TDM #1)

The Dragon's Need (TDM #2)

The Dragon's Bidder (TDM #3)

The Dragon's Charge (TDM #4)

The Dragon's Weakness (TDM #5)

WRITING AS LIZZIE ENGLAND

Her Fantasy

Holt: The CEO

Callan: The Highlander

Adam: The Duke

Gabe: The Rock Star

About the Author

Jessie Donovan has sold over half a million books, has given away hundreds of thousands more to readers for free, and has even hit the *NY Times* and *USA Today* bestseller lists. She is best known for her dragon-shifter series, but also writes about magic users, aliens, and even has a crazy romantic comedy series set in Scotland. When not reading a book, attempting to tame her yard, or traipsing around some foreign country on a shoestring, she can often be found interacting with her readers on Facebook. She lives near Seattle, where, yes, it rains a lot but it also makes everything green.

Visit her website at: www.JessieDonovan.com